Wounds Remain

A Novel

Yahne Sneed

authorHOUSE

AuthorHouse™
1663 Liberty Drive
Bloomington, IN 47403
www.authorhouse.com
Phone: 1 (800) 839-8640

© *2019 Yahne Sneed. All rights reserved.*

No part of this book may be reproduced, stored in a retrieval system, or transmitted by any means without the written permission of the author.

Published by AuthorHouse 12/14/2018

ISBN: 978-1-5462-7058-4 (sc)
ISBN: 978-1-5462-7056-0 (hc)
ISBN: 978-1-5462-7057-7 (e)

Library of Congress Control Number: 2018914107

Print information available on the last page.

Any people depicted in stock imagery provided by Getty Images are models, and such images are being used for illustrative purposes only.
Certain stock imagery © Getty Images.

This book is printed on acid-free paper.

Because of the dynamic nature of the Internet, any web addresses or links contained in this book may have changed since publication and may no longer be valid. The views expressed in this work are solely those of the author and do not necessarily reflect the views of the publisher, and the publisher hereby disclaims any responsibility for them.

Contents

In this book, you will find... xi
Introduction xiii

Chapter 1   The Start 1
Chapter 2   The Break 11
Chapter 3   The Milestone 20
Chapter 4   Where it All Began 31
Chapter 5   Can't Erase the Past 39
Chapter 6   The Intent 50
Chapter 7   The Unforgettable 60
Chapter 8   Into Her Life 72
Chapter 9   Happy Birthday 84
Chapter 10 Pandora's Box 95
Chapter 11 Set Me Free 101
Chapter 12 Moving On 109
Chapter 13 Knocking Down Walls 116
Chapter 14 Let Go 124
Chapter 15 You Are Mine 133
Chapter 16 You Will Be Missed 139

Thank you for buying a copy of my novel.

This journey has been a challenge but it has also been rewarding.

I dedicate my novel to everyone who has a dream and is too afraid to pursue it.

I dedicate my novel to everyone who has been told no, your dream is too big, you're wasting your time.

I dedicate my novel to everyone who needs someone to breathe life into their dream.

It took me eight years to fulfil mine.
I needed patience, faith, courage, and determination.

Your dream can be your reality.

If I can do it with the challenges I've faced,
I know you can too.

Just believe.

Mom:

Thank you for being my rock. Thank you for being with me during my journey from start to finish. I love you.

Lord:

You made a way out of no way for me.
There is not enough time in the world to praise you.

I am nothing without you.

Thank you.

Dimitri Reyes (Editor):

You have been wonderful
and are an amazing artist and person.

My novel wouldn't have taken form like this if it wasn't for you. You captured the details, big and small
while challenging me creatively.

May the Lord continue to bless you in everything you do.

Thank you from the core of my heart.

In this book, you will find...

Anger

A strong, uncomfortable, and hostile response to a situation. In this situation, the individual experiencing anger feels pain, hurt, or frustration and directs that energy towards their self or another person.

Bargaining

When a person reaches out to someone or the universe to make the pain go away.

Denial

The action of not believing something that is true.

Depression

One who experiences this sensation is filled with a sadness and regret that usually occurs when a sense of inevitability is realized.

Acceptance

An act of no longer looking backwards in order to move forward in hopes of trying to obtain the life one had. After the pain is calm, and a development of an understanding that there is a new beginning on the horizon.

"Age does not determine your maturity, it's what you learn from your experience that justifies your growth."

Yahne Sneed

Introduction

"The time has arrived Doyle and we have to go!" Madison said, as she started to pack my letters, notes, and awards into boxes she brought from her home.

"Look, my family and I love it here. We can't just go." I told her as I got up from my chair, slowly walking to her. She grabbed my hands and began to warn me about the big mistake I will be making. Not only to her but to the company if I decided to stay.

"If we're not going to leave together, then I'm leaving alone." She said this while dropping my award on the table then grabbing her bag. She gave me one final look and turned to leave.

I yelled, "Wait just wait a minute! Let's just say I agree. Where are we going to go?" I grabbed her arm that was closest to me and brought her in close.

"There is no place like Allentown that seems good enough to move my company and family."

"I know, but this is the 90's, baby. We have more opportunities now. And we need to think quickly." She said this with urgency in her eyes. I reassured her she was right.

"I will talk with my wife." I whispered to her. I looked into her eyes and I can almost read her mind.

"Doyle?" Madison said in a whisper of uncertainty.

"I know what you are going to say, but I need you with me." I cradle her in my arms. "You are coming wherever the company goes. She's my wife, she won't suspect a thing. I have her trust. She doesn't know that

I'm not in love with her like I used to be. I'll see you at 7?" I kissed her and looked into her eyes.

"I love every moment with you." She leaves the office modeling her hourglass shape as I stare at her red silk dress swaying and she clicked across the floor with her black heels that I love. She stopped at the door and looked towards the wall, touching a frame that had a picture of us the first day my building was finished with construction. "Mmmm," Madison sighs as she looks back at me, "we came a long way. This is not the end Doyle. Baby, it's the beginning." She turns to leave as I catch another glimpse of what I'll have forever. I sit down on my leather chair undoing the button of my black fitted Italian jacket. I look out the window for the last time. "A new start. A new beginning."

∽

Once, a long time ago called this place home but now most times I stay in the car after work longer than expected. I've had to build myself up to even go inside recently. Before leaving work I changed my shirt, and now I'm in the driver's seat with nothing but me and the car mirror's light. I brush my hair forward. *Smile,* I told myself when taking the last sip of whisky, still looking at my reflection in the side mirror.

"Honey, I'm home." I excitedly say as I open the door to the house. Antoinette enters the living room.

"Mmm... that's good." My wife says, leaning against the wall. As I hang my coat on the hook I looked around for other footsteps to greet me at the door. I proceed to question my son's whereabouts. To my surprise my wife doesn't know where he is at this time of night. I tell her that I'll deal with her later, and that I have other pressing matters to attend to that is much more important than being my son's keeper.

"Why do you have to be so mean?"

"Look, keep your emotional baggage to yourself. I have to get ready." I tell her walking upstairs into my room to find my suit and booze.

"Ready for what?" My wife says as she follows. "You have not been home in I don't know how long and now you leaving again?"

"Listen, lady." I turned around and paused. I felt myself getting upset, "This is for you all. It's a business meeting I have to attend." I tried to calm down but the thought of my woman pressing me to talk to her at this moment is not what I signed up for. I continued to pull out my suits to get ready. I pull out my favorite dinner suit, the black mandarin collar button-down shirt and black pants with my navy blue British style jacket. Last time I wore this suit I landed my big break that kick-started my own business. Madison was with me and I received so much support from her. She even thinks my navy blue suit is the reason for our rich future we are sharing together.

"Are you sure?" She asks trying to stand in front of me. She knows me too well. Though we've been distant, I still had to lie and sneak around.

"Now why would I lie to you?" I tell her and try to keep myself moving around to avoid her glance. She always wants to talk to me, about every little thing, and today is not any different. Her eyes pleaded with me. She rests her hands on my shoulders as I'm shuffling things around. I have things to do, but since I can't leave this house until I get dressed and Madison shows up, I might as well engage in some conversation to make my life easier.

"Fine, you want to talk? Okay, let's talk. We are going to have to move from here. My business is not going good as I hoped, the company and everyone else in it has to relocate. That means us too. ALL OF US. I have to go." I paused throwing my last pair of socks on the bed to look at her. I tried to hold my smirk, but the look on her face, well, it's priceless. I can't help to find humor in her dismay. I used to pay attention to these emotions but they only slow me down. Knowing I can get her this worked up over this minute situation brings me contentment. It gives me power. But I can't enjoy this too much. She's my wife after all.

"But wait I don't understand. Where to? How did this happen? When did this happen?"

"I was told about it today, and I don't have time to explain. My ride is coming. She's on her way." With all of these questions I continue to put my suit on in hopes not to be questioned about my private life.

But I see it in her face. Though I'm not in love, she is still beautiful. And I know what's coming from those lips, "On her way? Who is she?" Antoinette looks at me with praying hands to her face.

"Madison, okay? And don't ask me questions about her. I'm getting ready to see if I can fix what is left of my company's finances before leaving everything behind. Being a consultant for building firms has always been my dream. I can't…I won't stop now." I turn my back on her as I zipped up my pants. Why didn't you cook?" Trying to change the subject, but she's used to this.

"Wait. So your ex-wife is going to the meeting with you? Plus, you're getting all dressed up? What kind of meeting is this? Are there any other coworkers going?" Now she's pacing and I feel that her eyes haven't left me since I walked in.

"Excuse me? Baby. I am the one stressed out, okay? The company could go under. I don't have time to think about other women because I already have a beautiful one right in front of me asking me lots of questions, okay?" Tying my last lace, I stand up and hold both her hands to my lips. "I love you. Now, I am sorry that I yelled at you, but I am frustrated and tired." I turn to put on my suit jacket, "You can imagine how stressful it is to have to relocate my family and my business. Now be a dear, and stop questioning me." She gave me this look of uneasiness at first, but now it's starting to lighten up. I do well.

"I can help you look for houses." She said going to her laptop on her side of the bed.

"Okay great. Somewhere very far from this state.

BEEP, BEEP.

"Okay honey, that's my ride. Love you. Got to go." I walk over to Antoinette and kiss her cheek. I quickly walked away as I hear a faint *I love you* from behind me.

∼

I returned home from another breathtaking evening with Madison. She knows how to please me. I certainly know how to handle everything that I was leaving behind. Not only is she staying in my company, but she is also moving closer to me. I had to drive around to a nearby motel to clean Madison's smell off of me, and then drove around some more to let tiredness seep into me. Good thing it worked, now I look how I feel.

"Hey, I'm back." I said as I yawned and put my keys on the table. She was in the kitchen still on her laptop.

"Hey, honey. I didn't know what time you were getting home. Jahem and I ate, so I put the rest of the food in the refrigerator." I looked over at the refrigerator, then looked at her, then grabbed a tumbler from the cupboard.

"I.... I found a place to live, and I think you will like it." She walks to me with the open laptop with a tab of the house. I get water from the tap and she says, "It has the space you wanted, a great school for Jahem, plus, there is an opening for a job in my field."

"That sounds great honey." That word escapes my lying lips that once longed for her and loved to make her feel special. It could be my buzz but I felt myself talking before thinking or thinking and not talking. The drive and wild evening took more out of me than expected, I'm not as young as I was during my first marriage. I found myself walking upstairs very slowly, I wanted to sleep. Sitting on the bed, I take off my shoes.

"When are we expected to move?"

"At the end of the month." I felt her gasps. The discomforts of our prior conversation creeped back into my throat. "Yeah," I took a deep breath, "at the end of the month. I already called the vans. We have two vans waiting for the furniture and I got boxes coming in when we are ready to move. You and Jahem can start to pack this weekend. I'm going to bed." I said as I lied down.

"I know it's late, Doyle. However, are we not going to talk about this big move and this uprooting that is happening to this family?" She said with an attitude. "I am not waking him up. He doesn't know that we decided to leave yet!"

"Antoinette. If you're worried about Jahem, don't be. He is the next man in this house and he will adjust to the change." I struggled to get comfortable with Antoinette staring at me. I opened my eyes and looked at her.

"Yes, that is exactly what I am worried about Doyle. What about Jahem's friends? His… his school he loves so much? Have you thought how scary that'd be for him? A new school, new city, or state for that matter?"

"It's a change that I need to make to better my company." I sat up in bed and regulated my voice. I needed her to understand my passion to succeed. "Baby, if I listen to the emotions I have of being afraid or thinking I can't do this, then it won't happen. I have to do what is needed to be done for my company."

"What about your family? You should hold us at the same level as you do your company. I know your dad wasn't there for you like you would've liked, and you needed to prove that you can be successful. But honey…" she reaches for my hand and caresses it, "I believe in you. We will talk to Jahem together. He won't like this plan but we'll help him realize we're in this together."

"I'm tired." I removed my hand from her touch. "This meeting drained me. But I will say this, Jahem will be fine. My blood runs through him. So tomorrow you alone will tell him that we are moving. I have things I have to attend to for my company." I turn my back to her.

"Doyle, you've been drinking. I can see it, but okay, my love. Get some sleep." Her voice is quavering, as she begins to leave the room.

"Hold on," I groan, "Close the door." She turns around. I see her holding back tears but she obeys. I'm not having this crying while I'm going to sleep so I call her over before she finally leaves to grab her in my arms. I wish she was Madison but my mouth starts moving faster than my mind, "Baby, things will work out for the best now that we are moving. Jahem will just have to make new friends and adapt to the new change. We will all have to."

"Okay, get some sleep and I will talk to Jahem tomorrow."

"Thank you baby, I know I can always count on you. I love you, Antoinette."

Chapter One:

The Start

Jahem

It's March of my sophomore year and I already feel that school is almost over. I'm counting down the days until the summer and all I can focus on right now is that I am not from Wilmington, North Carolina. Inside I still belong to Allentown, Pennsylvania. I moved here at the beginning of the school year when my mom made the suggestion. She said it would be a good new start for mom, dad and I, "…Because of the different environment and setting." But I for one, know better. I think my dad got into a little dilemma over there in Allentown, and the only solution was to relocate his company from our comfortable Allentown to the overly friendly Wilmington.

My dad has a company called D n' M. I don't care for the name either. The "D" stands for his name, of course, but the "M" stands for his business partner, Madison. She's his first wife and I don't like her at all. She's the reason my father doesn't love us the way he should, and this pains my mother. Pains me. Of course D is in M. But that is much to the point of why she moved us to Wilmington. My mom is still with him, though we don't really get to see him anymore.

But if my mom wants to move, then we are all going to move. Allentown is a nice and pleasant town. It's quiet and everyone keeps to themselves while respecting one another. As for Wilmington, it's nothing I'm used to… it's different. Every time I turn around there are trolleys and tourists with cameras taking pictures in downtown. Wilmington has one of the best restaurants on the boardwalk. But nothing out matches the city's progressive culture and the Historic District. I have never experienced a whole town having such pride in loving where they live and this is what shapes Wilmington. I guess people love what they can't see every day, and that means my father fits right in.

I feel like a tourist when he's around. He never really had the chance to tour Wilmington but since he's so attached to the downtown district, he chose the downtown district to move and rebuild the company.

I like my solitude, but at the same time, the friendliness is what warmed me up to this new place. My mom seems to like it, as if she's been here before. She always tells me that I have to give it a chance. I gave it several long months and my feelings for Wilmington have changed some.

I still miss Allentown, but the summer is just around the corner and this town is growing on me and some things are similar, at least. Despite me not being picked on much back home, I still witnessed some fights and bullying and I'm not away from that here either, even if Wilmington is, "nicer."

But not all of it is. I start taking the back roads from the school to get home. This particular path always smelled of spoiled milk from the dumpster and it used to make me so sick. I eventually got over it, though. No matter how much things stink, you can learn to ignore it until one day you might just overcome it.

There's a large dividing wall that sections off the school property from the road and I have to pass in order to get home. Most days I feel myself hesitating to walk through, because on the other side I could always catch someone getting roughed up or jumped by some of the school kids. It became the norm until I saw them in ways I didn't know existed.

Over by the football field, they were wearing purple jean jackets with their collars pulled up and the words, "Tuff Boys" spray painted on their backs. As I walk up closer to them I notice that they were messing with a scrawny looking white boy that was trying to pop the lenses back into his glasses. Three of them were trying to count change and one of them was counting dollars. The one counting dollars was Colton. I think he's the oldest out of the group, standing about six feet two inches tall. His skin could be called Hershey's Dark Chocolate but it would be misleading, there isn't anything candy-like about him. He's very ugly, actually. His hair was oily, curly, and a dark brown, where his teeth were sharp and jagged. He had a crooked smile that became more distorted when he laughed hard at a joke that wasn't funny.

Then there's Jason, the pretty boy with all the moves. He's about five foot seven, and was the color of cocoa butter. He claims he is from India, but lived most of his life with his African father in northern Africa. He's the guy that thinks he can get every other guy's girl. The other three boys are brothers, two of them, Matthew and Izaiah, are twins. They're seniors and you could tell by their bodies. Light skinned, tall, and manly, I've seen them on the football field during gym. The last brother, Kevin, is a little smaller but also built, and following the example of his twin brothers.

Colton looks at me like I was going to say something and I stopped instead of walking by. I'm confused because this isn't like me, but I'm frozen. I want to say that the Tuff Boys is a very cheesy name for them, but of course the title, "Stupid" and "Ignoramus" probably didn't fit on their jackets, nor would they be able to spell them. That's what I wanted to say as more of them lock eyes with me but I didn't. Despite their lack of a dictionary they didn't need it for what they did to people. Last week, Colton hurt this kid for looking at him wrong. A kid in science class told me that in middle school, Mathew punched a kid in the gut for telling him to get out of the halls. The kid went to the hospital and refused to be the hall monitor after that.

They walk towards me. I can't take my eyes off of Colton's piercing pupils. Suddenly, I get real warm below the waist. I think its adrenaline, but now I feel it running down my thigh, towards my calf and collecting at the elastic of my sock. I PEED MY PANTS! I book for my house, running two and a half blocks and not looking back.

Luckily, my house is in running distance. Running up the stairs

I slam my bedroom door. Got out of my clothes and went to the bathroom to the shower.

It looks like I lost my chance to be a Tuff Boy, to make a name for myself. "They must think I'm a punk or something."

Even now sitting on my bed after taking a shower, I still think about Tuff Boys and how I can be one. My door cracks open and interrupts my thoughts.

"Dinner's ready, come and eat. I made your favorite, chicken, rice, and green peas." I smile, "Thanks mom." In the doorway, she's a little taller than me, and her voice reminds me of cocoa, like her skin.

I love her cooking. I sat in my chair and was preparing myself to chow down. As my mother fixed my plate she asks how my day went. I didn't want to tell her that I peed in my pants when I ran into the Tuff Boys, though that was the first thing that came to mind. She doesn't like them and she'd be *real* thrilled if I told her they punked me out. "Nothing happened, my day was normal." She's real good at catching a liar, though. She sees the look that I feel on my face and she knows it. I just look at her.

"Mom, nothing happened. Pass the butter please, my rice is getting dry."

Seeing that I'm not going to tell her, she changes the subject for the rest of dinner. "You know, Jahem, don't forget that I have to take you to the doctor tomorrow after school, so no playing soccer with your friends. Come straight home."

"Where's dad?" I asked as I turned into the living room to see if I by passed him on the couch.

"He's at work. He wanted to work over time." She's still forking at a few peas.

"With Madison?"

"Yeah, I guess. Just don't start." She scowls in a tired voice. As I started to speak about the injustice of not having a father or husband around, my mother gave me that look and asked me to do my homework, ending with the news that she'd have to speak with me later. I felt an uneasy feeling creeping into my lower stomach and unfortunately for me, I had no homework. Playing it cool though, I go upstairs to my room anyway. I think about the fact that my mother is defending my father while lying in bed. Eventually I told myself I no longer want to cloud my thoughts any longer so I got my books and clothes ready for tomorrow, and brushed my teeth. Heading back downstairs I was wondering what my mom wants to talk to me about. It'll probably go the same way that conversations about dad usually go. She's on the couch with a box on the table.

"Mom." I called to her.

"Come and have a seat, Jahem. First I want to say, your father and I have decided that you have grown. We were expecting to get you this gift for your birthday, but couldn't buy it in time. You are sixteen now and it's about time that you have more responsibility to get to different places."

"What? I'm getting a bike?"

"No silly, you're getting a car."

She handed me the keys with an Audi sign and we hugged. I was so happy I darted outside. Unbeknownst to me it was not there. Then she opened the door of the garage and there it was, a red 1998 Audi A4. Not my first choice in a car, but hey, it's not my feet that're going to be walking anymore.

I unlock the driver's door and go inside and marveled a console and dashboard that was mine. I let my mother in, "Well, do you want to drive it?" and excitedly I start the engine and carefully back out like she taught me. The car rides so smooth, wait until the kids at school saw me. I thought to myself, "Jason got competition." Going back inside I thank her again. It was 10:30PM now and I was tired. I said goodnight I went upstairs and went to sleep.

～

My alarm goes off and I disable it on my phone that reads Wednesday. Getting up to a stretch I catch myself saying in my mirror, "The girls are going to love me now." I make sure to drive up to school the exact time the girls get out from the school bus. I rode the car in front of the school bus and waited to catch a glance of one girl in particular sweet,

sweet Suesan. Suesan is also sixteen years old, tinted in a beautiful caramel with hips like an upperclassman. Suesan didn't necessarily have a model-type body, but she did have the right body. Someone told me once that she was a mutt. When I asked what that meant the guy said she was black, indian, and white. I wanted to tell him that she wasn't a mutt, that she was perfect. As the girls started to pour out of the school bus, I didn't see her.

"Hey Jahem, where did you get that car? Can I take a ride in it?" a girl from my right asks.

"Yeah sure you can, only for the best." Getting out of the car many girls from school had crowded around me. As I was talking to this beautiful girl with blond hair I hear another girl call out-

"HEY! QUICK! SUESAN COME LOOK AT THIS BOY WITH HIS NEW CAR." (No important girls really know my name.)

"What is your name stranger?" Suesan's best friend asks.

And I say in Suesan's direction, "Jahem. Jahem Thomas. And your name? Is it beautiful?" This car gave me extra courage.

"Johnson, Suesan Johnson. Nice to meet you, Jahem. I notice you got a car, is that yours, handsome?" I think she was flirting, but I couldn't tell if it was mocking me.

"Yeah, this is my car. Want to get in later?" I gestured to the door.

"Um...No, I don't think so." She says, quietly.

"Why?" I wonder. She's looking around nervous, not saying a word. "The car doesn't bite."

"No! It's just..." She trails off looking behind me and smiling.

"She doesn't want to hang around you. You think this piece of junk could win the girls, especially my girl." Colton walks around my Audi and puts his arm around Suesan. "You must be out of your mind." He says looking back at his crew coming out of the crowd.

"Hey Colton, isn't that the pisser we seen yesterday?" Jason said.

"Yeah, your right." Colton snickers. "Suesan, that's the guy I was telling you about on the phone, the one who peed on himself at the field. Ha! You don't want to be near this kiddie pisser."

"Yeah, later pisser." Kevin says as he gets pulled away by Izaiah. The first bell rings. Everyone turns away to go to the school.

"Damn man," I kick the tire to my car. "I lost the girls, most importantly I lost Suesan." I kick the tire again. "Damn, now how am I going to get them back?" I thought to myself leaning against the car.

"Hey, Jahem! Nice ride! What's got you down today?" DJ asked.

"Man, hey…it's just I got this car my mom gave to me." I look at the car. "I thought that might impress Suesan."

"Well, did it?" I can see he wanted what I just couldn't tell him.

"How bad is this one?" He asked leaning against the car with me.

"You remember Stacy and her ex-boyfriend Brad?"

"Yeah I remember."

"Worse than that." All DJ could do was shake his head. He continued to ask about her boyfriend while trying to cover his face from laughing. But when he felt my embarrassment he stopped.

"Her boyfriend is Colton from the Tuff Boys, bro."

"Daaaamn! You are in a shit hole now."

"Speaking of that." I said low.

"What did you do?" He squealed, then laughed really loud. I waited until he finished. In hindsight it's funny, but it's too soon for me to laugh.

"I kind of…" I look at him. "You promise you will not tell?" DJ reassured me he wouldn't tell. But the laughing, now that's questionable.

"Alright man, come on!" He yelled.

"Alright, yesterday when I saw the Tuff Boys messing with some kid after school, I was walking by, and Colton started staring me down." I put my head down preparing myself because I know he is about to laugh, I would've too. "Somehow I manage to pee on myself." I said in a whisper.

"Ha-ha!!!!! Dang man! How you do that?"

"Come on now, you said you were not going to laugh!"

"I'm sorry, but I said I won't tell. But you, now that's a laugh."

BING… BING.

"Come on man, today can't be as bad as yesterday."

How can I be mad at Doren James? He can laugh at me. We've been friends since I moved here. He prefers to be called DJ. He wants to stay cool just as much as me. And for a white boy, DJ is pretty fresh, and growing up in the 'hood helps. I'd compare him to Eminem, the same height and build. That's why some girls say he looks irresistible, with his blond hair covering his eyes. He's a good catch too, charming, smart, and could play it cool around girls. He tells me he doesn't have a girlfriend yet, but he likes some girls and some girls like him back, but he is always talking about how too young he is. He's not trying to settle down yet, but who is to blame him, life is too short to settle down when you're young. Right? That wouldn't be me but I respect him for it, he doesn't act like what he is not, and that's why he's my best friend.

∼

So I go to Clover High School. I'm in the 10th Grade, and at top of my class. I like where I am with my academics. It isn't too hard to have good grades here since everyone at this school seems to be afraid of being smart. Me, as well as Doren, Suesan and a few others will be doing something good with our lives. We all received a letter to skip a grade, but we all said no. We're taking our education like everyone takes everything down here in Wilmington, nice and slow. You can't rush education. I'm glad that Suesan is smart, because she is in two of my classes and it's a pleasure looking at her. For some time now, I've been staring and I know she knows that I've been staring. But I'm glad she doesn't say anything.

"Won't you just talk to her Jahem? You keep staring at the girl, she's not getting any younger." DJ whispers to me as I was sketching diagrams.

"What should I say to her?"

"Say anything but don't use any corny pickup lines." He smiles. "I'll move my desk over a little to give you privacy. You can do this." He pats my back.

"I tried to be sweet." I sounded defeated even in a whisper.

"No, you tried to be a player, playa. Try to actually be sweet to her. It might win her over." Boy, could he be pushy.

I stretch my arms towards Suesan thinking about what I should say. I got nervous and thought about pulling back. My palms are gross and sweaty.

"Um, excuse me, Suesan?"

"Hello. Are your hands clean?" She chuckles.

"Um..." looking at my hands. "Yes, they are." And my name is Jahem Thomas and I..."

"Yes, Jahem Thomas?" She cut me off making eye contact with me.

"I was wondering if I can get you a smoothie or something Friday after school?" I said this holding my breath which seems like forever. "Just as friends."

"I don't think that's a problem."

"Problem," I considered. "Um... what about your boyfriend?"

"Look, how about this. I'll meet you in the teacher's parking lot after school Friday and then we will go from there, okay, Jahem?" She says assertively.

"That will be great." I add.

"But one more thing, why not today?" She questions.

"Oh. I have a doctor's appointment..." She had that look of worry in her eyes similar to the way she gleamed by my car the other day. Oh boy, does she think I'm sick or something? I try to clear the air and assure her that I am not sick, and it's just a routine checkup.

"Oh, okay." She looks down on the piece of paper she had been drawing circles on since I tapped her shoulder. "Thank you. I haven't been treated to anything in a long time."

"Colton doesn't do anything?"

"No, not really."

"Do you even like him?"

"Why you in my business for?"

"I'm just asking..."

"Asking nothing! You better shut up before this date will be canceled!" Of course I didn't want that to happen. Silence is golden. And it's a date.

"Okay. Date. Friday. Parking lot." I return to DJ, and faked a smile of accomplishment.

"So what happen, Jahem?" DJ asked moving his desk in its original position.

I didn't want to tell DJ that I just got played by Suesan Johnson, so I just told him, I have a date. He starts asking all these questions about what I'm going to wear and say to her, as if I know how I pulled a yes from Suesan less than five minutes ago. I don't know anything about nothing, and I told him just as much. "I don't know DJ, but I know this, I'm not taking her home early. We could do some walking and a little bit of talking. So I can get to know her and she can get to know me." I say, excitingly, but inside I was very nervous.

"Excuse me, Mr. Thomas and Mr. James if you don't mind I would like to finish explaining about the Reproductive System." Miss Hanover said.

"Sure." As we both said in unison, but the bell rang.

BING… BING. As always, we were the last to leave and saved by the bell. Or so we thought.

"Can I talk to you, Jahem and Doren?" Miss Hanover takes off her glasses slowly, and looks at us. "Your interruption is not acceptable in my classroom, this will be the last time I warn you, okay boys?"

"Okay, Miss Hanover." We both look at each other grinning when she looks down.

I can't stand that teacher. Old Miss Hanover teaches Biology. Her classroom is big. Her voice is so low that people in the front can't hear her. It's very hard to stay focused when the teacher is talking low. Not all my teachers are like that. Let me tell you, first we got math, that's Mr. Cranford, a white teacher, teaches precalculus. He's not mean and we have a mutual respect for one another.

Then there's Miss Jordan, she's Chinese and strict. She teaches history. Next Ms. Cranny, she's very nice. She teaches English and she's Black. And then there's Mr. Benton, he teaches both gym and health. He has a fair class. Lastly, there's lovable Ms. Dias, she teaches Spanish, and I love Spanish just as much as I love her personality and spirit. This is a very easy class.

Chapter Two:

The Break

Jahem

The receptionist hands me some paperwork, "Alright, Jahem, sign these and the doctor will be with you shortly."

"Okay, thank you." As I pass my mother this stack of papers, I sat next to her to help fill them out.

The doctor's office is pretty big but not as nice as my hometown doctor's office. Even though this place did bring me peace, it was interrupted by a crying baby and the thought of me peeing my pants the other day. I tried to think about other things but I could only think about Suesan: what my date was going to be like, and how I'm going to work out this love triangle of chaos that seems to be developing. Not to mention, that I barely thought of how to dress, what to say, how to act, and where to take her. It was a lot to think about in a short amount of time.

She said yes to me because I was being me. I tried to convince myself I shouldn't need to be flashy for a girl that said yes. But this is Suesan, so… what should I wear???

"Jahem… Jahem did you hear me calling you, boy?" Mom squealed.

"Yes, ma?" And I snapped back into reality. My mom hands me the stack of papers to give to the front desk receptionist.

"Thank you, your new doctor is Doctor Bakim." She stated. "You can have a seat in the room and he will be with you shortly. There's just one more patient in front of you." After 15 more minutes of thinking about what jeans to wear on Friday, I hear a deeper voice.

"Alrighty then nurse, whom do we got here?" said Doctor Bakim, who stood taller than me. I noticed that he made my mom blush and stutter over her words. He had a deep smooth voice that vibrated when he laughed. I didn't like him too much.

"This is your new patient, Jahem Thomas and his mother Antoinette Thomas."

"How are you two doing today?" he said in friendly-doctor fashion.

Though I was a bit defensive at first, we both approve of his friendliness as we follow him into one of the back rooms. "If you don't mind, take off your shoes and step onto the scale…ok… 160 pounds…" he fiddles with his clipboard, "and 5 feet 7 inches."

"Great sweetie, you should join the basketball team or do some running." My mom says, looking up from her phone excitedly.

The checkup takes about 20 minutes and it went well. Walking to the car my mom asks, "What happened in school today?"

"Nothing really. I just asked Suesan out on a date."

"Doesn't she have a boyfriend?"

"Yes." I already knew where she was getting with this.

"And… she said yes?" I look at my mom. She looks very puzzled.

"Of course she said yes, why wouldn't she? Just because she has a boyfriend doesn't mean we can't go on a date."

"But you have to be careful, son. From what you've told me, he seems to have evil ways. I wouldn't want you getting into any trouble with what's-his-name if he found out." She said, concerned as she starts the car.

"Colton. And no mom, I don't think so. And you know something? She doesn't even like me so…"

"But the question is, do you like her?" She comments back quickly while backing out of the parking space as if she knew how I was going to respond to the whole conversation.

"Yeah, but I would like to get to know her more."

"Well, do you need any pointers on this date?" said my smirking mom. She looks at me and I feel bashful. "Well, do you?" her eyes are on the road.

"Well...yes I do. I do need pointers."

"Wait a minute, you never had a date before, have you?"

"No I didn't, ma." I hate when she puts me on the spot.

"I'm sorry son. I'll help you get ready for the date back at the house."

∽

Driving home I was thinking of all the ways I can get her to like me. I looked out the car window and watched the young couples as we drove by, I might get some last minute pointers by just watching. I should be romantic. I should shower her with care, flowers, and money. Just be plain nice. Just to think, a date with Suesan Thomas. It has a nice ring to it. I can't wait to see what waits for us in our future.

I walk all the way up to my room thinking about Suesan. I think about what my mom's advice is going to do for me as I prepare for a nice, hot shower. Heading to the kitchen I call my mom on the last step of the hallway stairs.

"I'm in the kitchen, sweetheart. Are you ready to discuss what to do?"

"Sure. What do I do?" This should be interesting.

"First thing you do is introduce yourself to her parents. Dress well and look presentable," she said, "let them know where you are taking her, ask for a curfew and a contact number. Say this with your back straight." She waved a wooden spoon at me. "And bring some flowers. Mixed Zinnias. Where are you taking her?"

"To dinner and then I thought of going for a walk by the boardwalk. We can talk a little then watch the comet pass." This sounded really good for someone who was just throwing out suggestions as he thought of them!

"Okay that sounds nice." My mom looks up as she thinks. "Second, take out her chair. Ask her what her favorite foods are and be polite. This is so you can order her food first and then yours." My mom says this while she precisely cuts onions. Her dating rules are as careful as her slices and I notice that she doesn't cry while cutting them. She turns around and doesn't say a word.

"Okay, is that it momma?"

"Yup." She turns to look at me up and down thoughtfully. "That's just about it." She returns to the counter and doesn't look back. I wonder if she is okay. "Oh, and you want to have decent things to say." She added, pausing her knife in the middle of her cutting.

"Yes, now that's the part I already know." I say, confidently.

I pause for a moment. The house was quiet with the two of us and I wonder why my father wasn't home yet. "I know you said to drop it mom, but where is he at? He hasn't called or come over yet?" I tried my best to sound reserved but was very puzzled. She resumes cutting the last of the onion.

"I don't know Jahem." She says, plainly. "Jahem," trying to change the subject, still with her back towards me, "take out the trash."

As I took the trash out, I can hear people from the school. I walk a little passed my house where I can see the school in the distance. There was a group of boys at football practice, they looked so much smaller from where I was. At our school, our team is named the Purple Clovers but right now they looked like purple specks. Most of the Tuff Boys are on the team. I know my mom wants me to join the running team next season, but girls like it more when you play football or basketball. I was on the soccer team at my middle school and it was received well but it's all about the ladies now.

Earlier on the drive home, I wondered if getting a spot on one of those teams would get me closer to Suesan. I mean, I'd treat her better and I definitely look better than Colton. I close and lock the door behind me and walk to my room after dinner with mom. My room is covered in blues, oranges and a king size bed that my father got me when we moved down here. I even have my own bathroom. I step into my walk in closet to get my clothes ready for tomorrow. Then I lie in my bed and drift off to sleep.

∾

I wake up to the light shining on my face. It's bright and earlier than usual on this Friday morning. Today's a different day and I get out of bed with a smile on my face thinking about Suesan. My mom calls me down to eat and as I got downstairs, he was home. He's built strong, not too muscular but you can still see his arms bulging slightly in his sleeves. I got my height from him and his light skin matched the football he held in his hand. He has flowers too, marigolds, her favorite. My guess was that he wanted us to forgive him or something. It's more of an assumption than a guess. He does this from time to time but I'm glad to see him. I decide not to show it though.

"Your mother told me that tryouts are approaching." He looks down at the football. "And I thought that I could help." He says this slowly still trying to say sorry.

"So what do you say, Jahem?" Mom looks at me, waiting for an answer. "Would you like for your father to help you?" I just looked at her and I felt myself give a *you can't be serious look*.

"No, that's okay mom, I'm good. I don't need him…"

BEEP… BEEP.

"That's DJ's mom. We're going to get something to eat then going to school. I don't want to take my car today."

"Alright Jahem." She says assuredly.

"Love you mom, got to go." Giving my mom a kiss on the cheek, I grab my house keys and head out the door and I didn't say bye to the man who gets credit for my existence.

~

"Hey Jahem, I see your dad is back." DJ says playing.

"NO, he's not my dad. Don't play like that. My father, not my dad." I tell this to him as straight as possible. He cautions me to chill and says sorry.

"Anyway, hello Ms. James. How are you?"

"Hello, Jahem sweetie. I'm doing good. And how are you son?"

"I've been fine, Ms. James."

"That's good sweetie." Ms. James said, as she makes a right turn from the corner of my house. Her brow is furrowed. I know she's concerned about my family situation.

"So Jahem, are you still nervous?" DJ asks.

"Nope, I feel better."

Doren and I continue to talk. On the way to Burger King, we came up by Suesan's house. She was wearing a baby blue shirt, white pants, white and blue KSWISS sneakers and a blue bow in her hair. She looks so put together.

"Hey man, what's wrong with you?" said Doren.

"Sorry man, I was just I…I-".

"I know, looking at Suesan." Doren says chuckling. "You got to stop that, you need to get a girlfriend and chill."

"Man, I'm not even like that and I know she's not like that!" Actually, I really wasn't sure about anything when it came to Suesan but I respected her enough to think she was perfect.

"Jahem and Doren, what do y'all want?" Ms. James asked.

As I was thinking, Doren says the number three and I say that sounds good too. We ate in the car but it was hard for us to drink so I waited. Doren on the other hand kept trying to drink the soda and then some spilled on the seats. He wiped it before she'd notice.

Driving closer to the school I see the Tuff Boys with Suesan and some other girls. I got out of the car and said bye to DJ's mom. We waited for the group to come by, I wanted to greet Suesan and the other girls. They say hi, even though I know Colton didn't want them to say anything to me. Colton grabs Suesan and snaps his fingers for the other T-Boys to grab their girls and then continue sauntering away. Doren patted me on the shoulders.

"Tough luck."

"I know man, no break." I say with disappointment. It's hard to talk to her when Colton is always interfering. Like Suesan needs his protection or something.

∽

We walk into Mr. Cranford's math class. I love math as much as

Spanish with Ms. Dias. In Mr. Cranford's class, I sit in the second row in the third chair. I prefer the first chair, but this will do.

"Good morning class, today we are going to take it slow since it's Friday. You have no homework but you do have class work."

We talk while we do our classwork. The announcements came on and I was in and out of it but paid attention when the reminders for tryouts were up. "Anyone that wants to sign up for football or basketball tryouts should give their name up to their respective gym teacher by lunch time today."

"Are you going to join the football or basketball team, or are you going to do what your mom says and join track?" Doren wonders.

"I think I'm going to try out for the football and basketball team. What about you?"

"I don't know. I guess I'll do the same."

Mr. Cranford calls DJ, Suesan, and myself up to his desk after announcements. He gives the three of us papers and asks if we want to skip a grade. We were his top three students and the only students to get perfect scores for the past two grading periods. I turn him down first and say that I didn't want to rush my education. Suesan and DJ agree.

After asking us several times if we were sure, he tells us he was pleased with our decision. Since we did not take the offer, he assures us that the positive energy we have about our education will go a long way. We sit down and finish our assignments early then we talk until the next bell rings.

The next time I see Suesan is in Ms. Cranny's class. She's one of the nicest teachers in the whole school.

"Alright class, can anyone tell me some of the similarities between the two assigned books? The first book being, *Thirteen Reasons Why* by Jay Asher and the other book being *The Perks of Being a Wallflower* by Stephen Chbosky." The teacher scans the room and sees Suesan's hand up. "Ah! Suesan! Go ahead."

Listening to Suesan's opinions of these books, I too started to reflect what similarities I perceived from the reading. It's a crazy idea to relate two books from different authors. However, sitting in my seat I relate to the characters in more ways than I thought.

I have always thought of myself as a wallflower and I don't mind the fact that I'm a bit of an outsider. Things become uncontrollable when too many people are involved in your business anyway, and I get that idea from Suesan's explanation of Asher. Suesan continues to walk the class through some of the book and I can't help but be drawn to her. Ms. Cranny responded to Suesan with a pleasing smile. "Excellent understanding of the novel Suesan. Is there any part of the novel that you connected to on a deeper level?"

Suesan took a while to respond to Ms. Cranny. She was in deep thought, but replied, "Yes. In many ways." Suesan points to the book in front of her. "*Thirteen Reasons Why* was an emotional rollercoaster for me. I connected to the main character and felt her need to not feel alone, and go through life feeling misunderstood." Suesan pauses and she lowers her head a bit longer than I expected her to. I couldn't see her face but I wondered if she's trying to hold back tears. Suesan continues to express her connection to the novel as if she has firsthand experience into the life of the main character. She mentions that *The Perks of Being a Wallflower,* holds a different connection for her as well. Fidgety in her chair, her hand was held high above her chest, "I appreciated this book for what it shared about the struggles of being a lone wolf. And how actions and mindsets change when having friends help you. With support and confidence in oneself, you can grow. For me, there is no greater feeling in knowing that friends can change a person for the better."

"That's good, Suesan! See, class? As long as you read the book you will be ready for the test this coming week." Ms. Cranny stressed, "You had over a month for both books. I suggest skimming through both again as a review. Please come to me during your lunch period if there are any questions."

I was thinking about how deep Suesan was when the bell rang and I was immediately reminded about afterschool. I can feel the momentum of the day continuing to pick up. The perk of finishing work early in class is that DJ, Suesan, and I are always among the first students to finish. So we've been talking more and it seems that Suesan is slowly coming around since I've asked her on our semi-official date. I'll take any amount of attention over zero. We all leave class and stop by our lockers. Suesan left quickly, rushing to her next class early. This gave me the perfect time to talk to DJ. I told DJ that I had a feeling that Suesan is more interested in me than usual, but it was hard to tell.

"Well, if you think she's interested, just make sure you play it cool. That, and hold your bladder." He smirked.

I punched him in the arm and chuckled as I picked up my gym clothes and headed to the gymnasium. This was the best class to me because it was super easy.

Walking down the halls I spotted Suesan in front of me.

"Hello Suesan." I greet cheerfully.

"Hello again."

"Um... How are you?" I hurried up to keep the same pace as her.

"Fine...Fine and you?" She hurried.

"What...um...class you got?" I was trying to get her attention.

"I got math." She pauses to look at me. "And you?"

"I have gym."

"Alright see you then, I'm late." She said as she cuts across the hallway. So hot and cold, I thought. "Bye, Suesan."

After gym came lunch. Sitting with DJ I can see Suesan with Colton across the room. Over cheesesteaks I say to DJ, "I just don't get it."

He sucks the grease from his thumb and grabs his soda, "I do. You're just a little jealous."

"Nah, man. I wouldn't call it jealousy. I just don't like her with him. I really wish she was with me but if she's happy with him, that's alright. I guess."

"Yeah, that's real noble and stuff. Personally, we both know his face looks like another one of his muscles." I laugh with him but I can't fully commit to it. She deserves my complete respect even if she's with Colton. All I know is, in a few hours, I'll be able to show her how a man should really treat a lady.

Chapter Three:

The Milestone

Jahem

At the sound of the last bell, I hurry to get my books and things to meet up with Suesan. My heart was pounding from the excitement of our date.

"So, Jahem, this is what you've been waiting for. Are you ready?" Asked Doren with a cheesy look on his face. Or was I the one cheesin'? Yet, it still seemed that he was almost happier for this day to come than I was.

"Yeah, I'm ready."

"Then when are you meeting her?"

"It was supposed to be right now."

"Alright. Well, I'm going to go and let you do your thing."

"Right. See you." We peaced each other out with our special handshake.

I locked my locker and headed for the parking lot to wait for Suesan. There she was sitting on the steps and reading a book.

"Is that the book we need to understand so profoundly like you?" I stare at Suesan as she looks up slowly from the novel. She closes the book and turns the cover of the novel in my direction.

"Yes, it's one of them." She pauses and stares at me. "Do you have a favorite book from this collection?"

"No, but I do appreciate both books."

"Agreed. You know, we can all receive a lot from these books if we look closely." We stare at each other and I can almost feel our thoughts resonating.

"If you're ready we can start walking to my car." I hold out my hand towards her hoping she will return with a touch but she wasn't looking. She put her novels in her bag and then slung it across her shoulder. Maybe I'll try again later. But I do grab her binder and notebooks that were on the step.

"What'd you do that for? I could have carried it. I'm capable." She reaches for her binder and I move back. She looks at me with those beautiful light brown puppy eyes again. I get lost in them and then I say, "I want to help."

"Oh," Suesan says, with a slow deep breath, "thank you." She grins pushing her hair behind her left ear.

"What, Colton doesn't carry your books for you?"

"No, not really..." Her grin went away. "He's the kind of person that will do it sometimes when you ask him, but he just doesn't think about it much. He does it when he wants to." She looks at me for a moment. "But it's polite for you to do so," she looks away. "That was nice." She grins again.

"Yeah, I'm a nice person, you'll see. I'm very attentive to those around me." I say nonchalantly, but inside I was losing it. I take a deep breath, start the engine, and begin to drive.

∼

It was silent for quite a while and I didn't have the music on. I forgot. When I turned on the radio the music in the car was filling up dead air. I felt kind of stuffy, and my palms were getting sweaty again.

"We're close to our hang out." That was the first thing that came to mind after several minutes.

"Where are we going?" I'm really glad she asked.

"First, we are going to eat at this delicious restaurant. This place is amazing. You are going to like it." I claimed while making the last left to our destination, "Then we will take a nice stroll on the beach."

I looked at Suesan in what I hope was sly and cool. I leaned over to whisper, "Do you know what else we will be doing tonight?"

"Suesan looked at me and for a while. I didn't understand why her face read, *ew*. Her nose turned up as if she smelled something sour. Suesan moved her head slightly away from my face. "No I won't guess because I already know. And I will not make out with you because we are on a date."

"No! That's not my intention!" I said shockingly. "What made you feel that way to even say that?"

"Let's be real, Jahem. Every guy wants to take their date out, and after the date, they are looking for something more than food and conversation. Or at least they're thinking about it." She said seriously. "You telling me that's not true?"

"No Suesan." I looked at her when I parked the car. I know that eye contact is key. "Maybe you haven't met the right kind of guys." We started to get out of the car. Man! This date was already getting blown out of context. "Girl, all I was going to say was there was going to be a comet passing through today and we'd be able to catch it while we were out. Nothing to do with making out or anything like that." She gave me this certain look that threw me off. I couldn't tell what she was thinking. We continued to stroll.

"WAIT!" She stopped walking and this made me stop. "Sorry." She sighed. "It's just that all guys I've been around… When we're together… They just want that." She said, switching from biting her bottom lip to her top lip.

"Well I don't, I just want to get to know you better. Is that alright?" She didn't respond, but softly smiled. I took her hand and it was soft. We continued to walk. "It's just around this corner."

"I know this place," she said surprised, arriving to the entrance of The Groove Room. "I used to come here all the time for family gatherings." She said happily.

This spot is on Lumina Avenue off of Wrightsville Beach. I felt like this was a very classy place because it carried wine. We couldn't have it, but it was a beautiful atmosphere: dimmed lights, candles, and The Groove Room was known for their pasta and bread.

"Welcome to The Groove Room. Do you have a reservation?" The hostess asked.

"Yes Ma'am, I do. A table for two. The name's Thomas."

"Okay great! Right this way sir."

Following the waitress, I observed how many people there were. I dodged a bullet by making a reservation. That would've been embarrassing if I hadn't.

The hostess guided us to our table with a good view to the stage. "Here are your seats. Enjoy."

"Thank you." I said to her as I quickly advanced to Suesan's side so I could pull out her chair. I looked at Suesan and motioned to the chair, "After you."

"Thanks." Suesan politely said sitting down.

I took my seat. "On Fridays there's a live band. See them setting up now. It's great I reserved our table."

"Wow, I've never been here on a Friday. It seems like you really thought about this." Suesan was all smiles. Great, I was bouncing back!

Our waitress arrived after some time. "Hello, my name is Shauna and I'll be serving you today. Do you have your order ready?"

"I'm almost ready, are you?" Suesan looked at me as if she memorized the menu.

Looking at the drinks I couldn't help but feel my face contort at the prices. I never looked at them much going out with mom and my father. It's real different when you decide to pay yourself. I think Suesan and Shauna could see my face change but I didn't want to look up.

"While he's still deciding you can take down my order." Susan said, "I'll get the grilled chicken and potatoes with onions and gravy."

"That's a popular one. And what would you like to drink?"

"A ginger ale for me."

I followed up, "You know what? I'll just have the same."

"Perfect, I'll get these drinks for you shortly." Shauna grabbed our menus and walked away.

When she was gone, I returned to Suesan. "So tell me, what's this with you and Colton?" I was dying to know and I tried to say it with some concern, but it truly made me boil inside. Anyone that likes him is very troubled and that made me nervous. Besides, every time he's mentioned she has this look that is unpleasant and distant. Her eyebrows crease and her breathing becomes shallow. If I didn't know any better, it looked like she was going inside herself.

"I like Colton because he is sweet. All of that hardness he tries to put out, is a front." She said this fumbling with her utensils.

"Well, by what you tell me, it seems like Colton is not who he makes himself out to be. Especially to the rest of the school and the neighborhood."

"He has his moments." She looked at her reflection in the silver spoon.

"I don't know. I'm sorry, but it's a bit hard to believe." I crossed both arms as I put them on the table, leaning over slightly as if I was telling her a secret I'm sure she already knows. "You need him to be sweet all the time. Not just when he feels like it or when he's in a good mood or nobody's around."

"I know…" She paused and was looking directly at me. By this moment those light eyes were piercing my soul. Still beautiful, they now looked cold and angry. "But to be brutally honest, you need to stay out of my business."

I leaned back again for distance. Maybe I was coming on too strong. "Okay, chill out Sue. I'm sorry. I didn't mean to get all in your business. I just…" Leaning back even further I was trying to give off the impression that I was relaxed. "Just relax and we'll start this conversation all over again, alright?"

"Yeah…Yeah okay." She said, still apprehensive but coming back to some calm.

"Alright." I let out a big breath that I hoped would act as a restart button. "So, how many brothers and sisters you have?"

"I have two eight year old brothers, one twelve-year-old sister and a three year old baby sister." She said this looking around the entire room, observing everyone that walked through the entrance. "And you?"

"I have no siblings. I'm the only child. My mom was going to have another child but…"

"But what?"

"Prob-"

"Hi, are you all ready?" The waitress asked coming over with the food.

We both expressed our gratitude and then Suesan turned her attention back to me. "So back to you, Jahem. You were talking about problems your mother had with having the baby? Is that too personal?"

"No, it's okay." I said this not really wanting to tell the story, but I felt that if I opened up like this, we'd be having a real conversation. Mom said I should have meaningful things to say. "My dad was always gone and my mom figured she couldn't raise two kids by herself. My mom told me when I was younger she was going to have another child but believed her husband wouldn't stay with her if she did. He stayed of course, but that means I never got a brother or sister."

"That's just awful. A woman is always at the beck and call of a man." Suesan put her head down and started to play with her fingers in between bites. During the time I spent with Suesan, I could already begin to tell when she was getting upset and when she was happy. I didn't know where to take the conversation, so I stared at her and waited. At times, she looked like a painting out of our English textbooks, like one of those in the side panels that read *oil on canvas*, except there wasn't anyone in there that looks like her. The pigment of her skin, melanin brushed on her arms and cheeks, freckled in the patterns of salt crystals in waves. Every image of her does something to me that I can't explain.

She looked up and I couldn't snap out of this silly trance. Then she looked at the waitress when she came to check up on us. She said she was fine, and I asked for a refill on my drink, but then I went back to forgetting how to speak. She seemed used to putting up walls and I wondered of her insecurities. I saw that even when she was having a good time she wanted to pull away. I started to fiddle with my utensils and sip my drink then I thought of a way to continue.

"Well Suesan, as you already know, I'm new to this place. I haven't exactly got used to living here."

"No, Jahem, I didn't know that. Far as I knew you lived here your whole life, you just decided that you wanted to come to this school. I figured you were home schooled or something."

"Really? Yeah, well it's true. This place is okay, but I kind of miss it back where I was before."

"Where is that exactly?" As she sat up in her seat with growing curiosity.

"I'm from PA. It's a nice town. Allentown. Ever heard of it? I'm going back there during the summer."

"So how long have you lived in Wilmington? Since the start of the school year?"

"Yeah, we moved down last summer. And you?"

"Just my whole life."

"Have you ever been to Pennsylvania at all?"

"No, I had never been there. How is it?"

"It's better than here. Take every good thing that Wilmington has to offer and multiply it by 5. That's how I feel about Allentown."

"I can say that is a nice place then?"

"Yeah, but I like here too." I said as I stretched my arms to Suesan's side of the table.

"Why?" She said laying her hands about 6 inches from mine.

"Because," I looked into her eyes and spoke before I could think, "y-you." I'm stumbled over my words, "Because of you."

"You don't mean that." Suesan looked like she wanted to move her hands away, but she didn't.

"But I do. I really do." Suesan said that it was a nice gesture, but it didn't seem so great since she refused to look in my direction. I was realizing that this girl was unbelievably tough, but I couldn't give up. I continued to look in her direction. She switched the conversation.

"So, is your mom planning on having a child now?"

"Well as of right now, she decided to just stay with me. I think she is afraid that she'll get left high and dry again like he did the first time. They were both young. My father comes and goes now. He always has business trips to nowhere. Supposedly he moved here to have a present life, but he's gone even more than he was back in PA." I said this rubbing the back of my neck. "If you ask me, I think that my father is cheating on my mom."

"Why you think that?"

"My father's secretary is also my father's ex-wife. I heard once that they divorced because of his ex-wife's father. But her father is dead now, so I guess that doesn't stop Doyle from much." I clenched my teeth together at the thought of Doyle being so deceitful to my mother.

"Wow, okay. Well when you put it that way, I can see why you feel the way you do. What about your mother? How does she feel about it?"

"My mom trusts him a lot, and that's the sad part." I sighed when I noticed how concerned Suesan looked. "You don't have to feel bad for me. This is just petty stuff. My mom and I are alright." That was me attempting to reassure her.

Suesan's face looked a bit different than it had when we first left school. "And all this time I thought you were stuck up." She said with guilt but a bit of humor in her voice. Maybe even relief?

"Is that why you've been like this towards me the whole time? The attitude? The rudeness?"

"Well I wouldn't necessarily say attitude, but yeah. I figured you were already feeling some type of way with your fancy car and such. And you're pretty cute so I thought you were kind of conceited. That's why I had not been open with you but it always seemed easy to. Who I thought you were made me not want to not say anything to you." She continued to fork potatoes into her mouth.

"It's okay, I'm not here to harm you in any way. I hope you realize that." It's amazing that she even made eating look heavenly. Her long, long hair was pushed back and the candlelight shimmered in her eyes and they almost looked on fire. But not of a destructive force, on the contrary, it revealed the most beautiful representation of peace anyone would ever see. I could live in the comfort of her eyes and hair if it meant Wilmington would be my new place to call home. As mom always says, home is where the heart is, and the heart and home are moving closer together.

I noticed the music from the band was a jazz version of some pop song I heard on the radio the other day. Something told me to ask her to dance and before I can ask her, she said, "OOOOH, I love this song! Do you want to dance?" I laughed to myself and took her hand as I ushered her to the floor. We started to dance and I got a whiff of her hair as she was cutting the wind with her hands and hips. She smelled like strawberries. We grabbed hands for a bit and continued to rock. What started out as dancing apart led to us being pretty close. We were side by side, step by step, everything was going perfect. Then all of a sudden she's looking up at me as I'm looking down at her and I can't hear the music. I forgot all about The Groove Room, my dad, Colton, my pissed pants, grades, Allentown, and at that very moment we lean into each other and slowly kiss a soft and tender kiss. It's like soft pillows. And we kissed forever. She pulled herself away from me and stopped dancing.

"Did I do something wrong?" I asked sweating.

"It's not right, I'm with Colton. This is so not right." For the first time, she was still holding my hand while she held her forehead with the other. "I'm sorry, this just isn't right. It feels like I'm cheating."

"It's okay, I understand." I reassured her. "Let's finish eating.

After we ate, we still talked for some time until I asked for the check.

∼

I thought about our entire dinner-date while we walked by the beach. It's about 5:30. I knew the stars were slowly starting to shine bright. I walked through this beach plenty of times to think, I believe it could do us some good to not be around that many locals. It's the end of the school year and within a few weeks, I'm sure the boardwalk will be riddled with out-of- towners. The smell of sea salt and clams soothes me better than P.A. A bit darker now, the crystal blue water starts to shine as the sunset kisses the horizon. It puts Suesan under a type of light that makes her look angelic as we find a spot away from the surfers and fishermen. We kick off our shoes and put our feet in the sand as we sit near the docked boats to the left and the open shoreline towards the right. I felt the wind picking up and noticed Suesan was looking a little stiff so I zipped up my hoody and took off my jacket to put around her like I've seen people do in movies.

"Thank you."

"You're welcome."

"I live so close to this beach but rarely come."

"Welcome back. And now you get to share this time with someone."

"Jahem?" She pauses. "The only reason that I'm going out with Colton is for protection. Protection from other girls at school and on the streets."

"What you mean?"

"For some reason, everyone feels that I think that I'm better than everyone else. And I don't. I have no clue why. So to have them leave me alone, I told Colton that he can be my boyfriend. But he's my protection. I'm not running, but I just don't want to fight. I feel tired and lost. So yeah, I feel like I need him."

I didn't say anything. It wasn't a time to speak, and I didn't really know what to say. We both thought it was a good idea to text our mothers, we knew it was getting late. We've been out on the beach for a while now and I believed Suesan was warming up to me because she starts to rest her head onto my shoulder. To play it cool and not get too pushy I didn't react though I just wanted to hold her and kiss her again.

She continues to speak and says how she doesn't want to really be with him, but no one will bother her as long as she's with him. Her life at home hasn't been swell either. Her parents started getting into a lot of arguments when she was thirteen, "At night I will hear them on the other side of the door...When my mom doesn't give in to his demands my dad leaves and won't come home for a day or two. Lately, it has been a little better." I didn't want to interrupt this moment but the comet was going through the sky. I nudge her and point up Suesan followed my gaze and we both admired the small and shiny stripe moving through a purpled and orange sky.

Soon we start to walk to her house, and as we turn on her street, she gives me back my jacket.

"Thank you for a nice time. Colton or anyone else for that matter never did anything for me like that. I had fun."

"You're welcome, but you don't have to thank me though. I had a great time. I'll see you in class on Monday…" I start to walk, but her hand touches mine.

"Jahem… Wait." She says hesitantly.

"Yes Suesan?" I quickly turn around.

"Can I ask you something?" I'm holding her hands now.

"Can I have a… kiss?" I couldn't believe she wanted another kiss! But who am I to disagree?

I reach for Suesan's waist slowly. She lets me and I pull her close to me. I kiss her with the most amazing feeling beating in my heart. She runs her hands on my shoulders and places her fingers tips light on my burning ears. I press her against the bricks of her house and she pulls me in. Suddenly, I taste grilled chicken and potatoes and smell an intense aroma of strawberry. It seems the stiff cold has disappeared and the night has invited warm air. Just then, lights flash from behind me as a car zooms past and the vibration of a muffler stops us.

Coming back to the present moment I felt an uncertainty in my manhood that I did not notice before. I'm glad I stopped kissing her, there's no telling where this moment could have taken us. I didn't know if that rush of blood I felt was regret or love. I know I wouldn't control this situation in this manner. Especially knowing that she's in a vulnerable place right now. I back away breathing slow but heavy as I stared at her while leaning against her porch. I fix her hair that I so passionately tangled in our unforgettable moment. She fixes her shirt.

I put my hands on her shoulders. "Suesan" I can't find any words. I could barely think.

"I know." She says as she found my eyes. Even in the streetlights, they shine bright. "Have a nice night, Jahem." She says quietly.

"And you do the same Suesan, take care." I say this as she walks to the front of her house and unlocks her door looking at me one last time before walking in.

As I left from her doorstep towards my car. The cold quickly grabbed me again.

Chapter Four:
Where it All Began

Doyle

It's the winter of 1976 and I'm home looking over my plans for my dream business. A company that I can call my own. My father has a business but he doesn't show me the ins and outs about how he makes a living. All I know is that he brings home lots of money and demands respect. This is where I want to be sooner than later.

The storm knocks down a tree in front of my house and it distracts me from my work just for a second. I walk over to the window and look at it, a broken oak with a circumference so large it took up a whole parking space. Luckily it missed the cars that are in my neighbor's driveway. I turn back to my plans and suddenly don't feel the same strength pouring out of me. How could a tree so rooted, strong, and visible be knocked around by the whispers of an unseen wind? Who am I kidding? I don't believe I will be able to own my own business and not answer to the white man, look at my support system. My mother married my dad because she needed a way out of living with her drunken parents, she doesn't ask for much. I know my mom struggles, and sometimes she opens up to me about her parents. All I know is I don't want to be like her, her parents, or my father. I told myself I don't want to become them. I am their child but I'm to focus on my love for power and money. I'm hoping that one day my business will flourish into something full of wonder.

I start to erase my work off of the whiteboard. I have to make more edits to my business plan; bigger, bolder and better. I want to make a statement to the white man. Therefore, in order to be a consultant I have to dream big and start small. I have to keep planning and drawing. I must've spent hours and hours. The day went from a daylight blue to an afternoon purple and the more intensely I heard the wind, the faster I worked. Many hot chocolates later, my sketches become what I want them to be. Powerful.

Suddenly there's a knock coming from my window, maybe a piece of hardened snow but then another and another. I look up from my beautiful creation to see about the noise. I open my window and in the whirring gust, I look down to see my girlfriend Madison, covered in snow and waving. I grab the ladder that I made on the days I wanted to leave the house without my parents knowing and place it out the window.

"I have the ladder secured." I yell down to her, holding the ladder tightly as she climbs.

Madison reaches the top and I grab her hands, pulling her over. She has a basket around the seat of her elbow with a plastic bag on top. I go to my dresser to get her some dry clothes and she shuts my window cutting off the howling of the snow storm.

"What were you doing outside? You could have killed yourself. It's bad out there."

"Oh shut up. That storm has so much intensity." Madison says sounding almost aroused. "Isn't it strange that even nature can represent force and concentration?"

"Concentration?" I ask as I give her my sweater.

"Yes. It knows where, how, and when it wants to go, then it does just that. I love it. It excites me."

As she changes I begin to unload the basket and I see she brought us dinner from home. Coated fish, fresh vegetables, brown rice, and delicious thick lamb with a special surprise.

"Really? Hippie weed, Madison?"

"Oh, don't tell me you don't like smoking anymore. What happened? Did your parents tell you to stop? I thought your parents don't pay enough attention to you?" Madison starts to laugh as she takes the weed from me, but I take it back from her and light the damn thing myself.

"My parents don't stop anything I do. And speaking of parents, didn't yours say you can't be around me anymore? My parents don't like you and your parents don't like me."

Madison walks over to me sitting on the bed. As she straddles me, I blow a puff of smoke and she takes the joint from me and pulls.

"My parents are not going to stop me from being with you. I love what you stand for. You are going to do great things. And I will be right there supporting your every move." Madison blows the smoke in my face and kisses me.

"I love your energy."

"I love your power." I shake my head. Even though I've worked on my business plan forever, I didn't feel so powerful.

She lifts my head up to meet hers. "With my help, you'll be as powerful as you want. I see that in you."

"I can't wait for my company to start bringing in money. We're going to have kids and-"

Madison puts her pointer finger on my lips. "Doyle. We are not having kids." She's serious and the look in her eye is deadly. Once I am lost in them they begin to soften in tone. "Why have kids, when we can have all the money we want? I just want you."

We make out and continue to smoke until we felt like eating. We spent the rest of the evening talking about our life plans and she loved our ideas about life and business. After that, we did things our parents wouldn't approve of but that's fine, they were busy.

∼

I woke up the next morning to Madison gone from my arms along with her belongings. This is normal but every time she leaves me alone, I feel a bit empty. I called her all morning but only spoke to her voice mail. Also normal. I stayed in the house to finish looking over loans and funding resources that'll help me with my start-up. At age 22, there are not many people that will help me because I'm a liability. I probably spent hours staring at the wall and I thought about college. I didn't apply to any colleges because Madison had convinced me that it will take too much time away from focusing on my dream. I know she is right, but without any money, I can't live the life I want.

My friends call me to hang out with them, I look at the clock and it is about two in the afternoon which means I just sat here for three hours. I haven't been anywhere in a long time because I am always with Madison or at home so I thought this was a good time to go out. I met my friends at this lounge we'd go to because all of the ladies in the neighborhood liked to drink there. My friends left me at the door to find chairs for everyone but I went to get all of our drinks on my father's credit.

I asked the bartender, "Hey, can I get four beers please?"

"I wouldn't make you out to be a beer person." Said a different voice.

I turned to my left to see her beautiful eyes resting on mine. Her smile warmed my heart and I was frozen in them so I couldn't do anything but stare at her.

"Or maybe it is. Never mind."

"No. It's, it's not. But everyone drinks it, right?" She looked at me as she took another sip of her drink. "Um, hi. My name is Doyle. It's my first time I'm seeing you here. Are you new?"

"Yes. I recently moved here a month ago. I'm Antoinette but you can call me Anna if you like." Anna held out her hand for me to shake it and I did just that. She was so soft to the touch and her scent was sweet as cocoa butter.

"What brings you to this side of town?"

"I work for a company that helps better teachers in the classroom. I am the one who advocates for student education and travels to different areas to provide better services for the teachers and students. So I'm here for a couple of months then I'll be sent somewhere else."

"Oh, so you're not permanent?"

"Doyle, nothing is permanent. You make it what you make it."

I stared at her and she stared back. She's fascinating. The bartender puts the four beers in front of me on a tray. I looked at the beers then back at Anna.

"How about I give these drinks to my friends over there and I come back to you so we can talk more about how we can make more out of this situation. What do you say?"

Antoinette sipped the last bit of her drink and looked at me seductively. She turned to me and whispered in my ear. "Deal."

∽

Three months later and I still find myself still in the arms of Madison. She set up a meeting with one of her father's big funding partners who invests in new projects every year. Somehow Madison convinced her father to choose me for a potential investment this year. I don't know the details but I have so much I owe to Madison.

After my appointment with him, I left the meeting feeling ambiguous, Madison's father wasn't one to express much emotion.

I arrive at Madison's house to be greeted by her with two glasses of champagne and a box of chocolate covered strawberries.

"I just received a call from daddy," she paused, "and he said you got the money to start your business!" She shrieks as she gives me a hug. "Here, this glass is for you. Come in, come in. Let's go to my room. My parents aren't here."

"Madison," I call to her as she opens the door to her room. "How did you get your father to meet with me? I thought he didn't want us together?"

"Oh. That was easy." Madison says as she fans her hand at me to sit on her bed. She really likes her champagne. "Daddy still thinks we're not together. I told him it's the least we can do for not getting his blessing." Madison chuckles. "He totally fell for it. I got him wrapped around my finger. He'll do almost anything I ask him to."

"I thank you, Madison." I walk over and bend down to give her a kiss. I gulp the last bit of my drink.

"Slow down. We have more to drink."

"It's okay. I'm not much of a drinker."

"Well," Madison thinks to herself, "try it with me. Let's drink this bottle and see how we feel." She gets up from her bed, goes downstairs, and returns with two of her father's dark liquor bottles.

"I'm okay really. I just want to chill."

"So after everything I have done for you, you don't want to celebrate with me?" Madison walks over to a glass on her table and fills it to the top. Then she turns to me. "If you want to be a powerful man like I know you can be, you need to see how much you can handle. You have to be ready for anything life presents you. Trust me, all of the worries and doubts you have inside of you will leave once you have this."

"But my mom's parents. She warned me-"

"Your mom's parents are not as strong as you. They were drunks. I won't let you drift that far from me." She kisses me on the lips then on the neck. "I'll always be here. You are in control." Madison picks up the glass and places it in my hands.

"Okay. I trust you." I start drinking with Madison. I don't like the taste at first, but after a while I start to like it. So much so, that whiskey is becoming my favorite drink.

∼

"Hey stranger. I haven't heard from you in over a week. How have things been going for you and your new business?"

"It's going great, Anna. Everyone is impressed by what I've planned. I can't wait until it's finished. I found a place to build my company and with this new deal going through I can help them make sure their building is steady and strong. I was told that it will happen in a couple of months, until then I'm still working under someone. I wish you can stay to see this really take off."

"I leave at the end of June. But why do you still need me around? You're with Madison."

"I know. But I can't help how I feel about you. It's not about the sex either, Antoinette. You help me see things differently. You help me to be a better person. Do you want children, Anna?"

"Why is that important Doyle?"

"Please answer me."

"Yes. Yes, I do." Her answer pulls at my heartstrings. "Why?"

"It's nothing. I don't want you to go."

"You have a girlfriend and a dream to fulfill. I have my career and you know I didn't go to school. You already know my plan, this is paying for college and once I'm done, I'm going to teach. This is how I can truly help children, not just teach teachers how to help them. And I can't do that if I stay here."

"Your dreams matter to me, Anna. I will just enjoy your company until you leave in June. See you in a little while."

I walk to the liquor store to get my bottle of whiskey and take sip after sip until I reach Anna's hotel. In the lobby I'm hugged from behind. It was Anna.

"Hey, I didn't know you'd be here this early. I was just setting up. I brought some whiskey. Let's have a drink."

"Doyle." Anna says as she lets go of me. "I don't need to drink in order to have fun with you. I don't like to drink that much. When did whiskey become your drink of choice, anyway? When I met you 6 months ago you could barely throw back a beer, let alone hard liquor."

"It just happened. It snuck up on me. I just drink to calm down. I am in control."

"Do you need help?"

"No. I'm not weak."

"Needing help doesn't make you weak. Not seeking help does."

We watch some TV and speak about our jobs but I can tell she isn't too happy with me. Anna and I end up holding each other and not having sex. All night I feel conflicted as I watch her sleep. Conflicted about what power and pride really mean. Is my definition wrong?

I wake up to Anna opening the door to the hotel's room service. The smell of coffee and bacon is wonderful. We both ate then washed up and went outside for a walk through the park.

"I am happy you drove over here to visit me instead of me coming to you. I really did miss you Doyle." Anna kisses me and I can't help but feel how different it is from Madison.

"I missed you too. And I always will. Where are you moving to next week?"

"Maryland, the seafood capital." Anna's face turns serious as she walks me over to the nearby benches.

"Doyle." She pauses and taps her fingers on her leg. "What do you want after you are established?" She turns to listen to my response.

I pause too. "I don't know. A family I suppose."

"Don't spend your whole life waiting." I look at her and grab her hands. She moves her hands away and that cocoa butter smell leaves.

"Not even for me or for...Madison. You asked me if I wanted children. Is it because of her?"

I sigh deeply. "I did." I sat back on the bench. "I think I'm going to marry her. I owe her that much. We're both running the business together and we both love the power and control. I believe she's my other half." I look towards Anna who is silently crying. "Oh. I didn't mean to hurt you. You're moving. Real soon. And I just...Madison is here. Please don't cry. I love you." Anna looks at me as fresh tears fall from her eyes.

"What did you say to me?" She looks up, I wipe her eyes and kiss her wet lips.

"I said I love you, Anna. I love you." We kiss again and I hold her, whispering softly into her ear, "I'm so sorry you can't stay. I love you."

Chapter Five:

Can't Erase the Past

Doyle

I receive a letter under the door when I arrive back from our honeymoon in Hawaii. I go into our room to read it but Madison comes in and jumps on top of me. She throws the letter on the floor and starts to romantically kiss me.

"Can we at least unpack and enjoy each other's company before we start to make love?"

"We can enjoy each other's company while we make love." Madison smiles widely as she reaches under the dresser and pulls out a bottle. "Let's have a toast for making it back safely as husband and wife. We didn't have a proper wedding because we couldn't, so this is our time to celebrate." Madison sits on my lap and pours our drinks.

"Okay. I'll drink to that." I take the cup in my hand and race Madison to finish. This has been our unofficial drinking game for several months now. There have been times where we can go through two whole bottles in a night playing this game. I usually win, of course. Over the last year, I have been very skilled at drinking liquor fast, and I'm proud of it. I am still working on holding my liquor but Madison says it will take time. So I will keep trying.

At the last gulp of the bottle, Madison nibbles on my ear and says, "Now that that's over, I want to enjoy your company inside of me." We made love for the rest of the night and eventually popped another bottle. We lavished in each of our bodies and alcohol until we passed out.

We wake up the next day both late to work. Madison's father spots us both with a hangover and calls Madison into his office. Through the glass room, I can see how their conversation is becoming more intense. Her father was aggressively slamming his hands on the table and I observe that the glass room is not as soundproof as it is said to be. I came to Madison's rescue. As I start walking toward them, primping my shirt and straightening my tie, her father stares at me with that same deadly look that Madison has when she's upset. I open the door, tall and with my head high.

"If I find out you had anything to do with my baby drinking, so help me I will take everything you love and make you wish for mercy!" He was changing color. I look at Madison then back at her father as I was examining the situation, but really I've wanted to speak to him for a while.

"She is not your baby. She is your child but she is also an adult. I didn't make her do anything that she didn't agree to." I see the look in his eyes and Madison did too. It's the look that gives the phrase, *if looks can kill, I would be dead*. I know he doesn't like me and all I can do is stare at him and not break my focus. She steps in and tells me to walk away. After a long stare down I leave and walk to my office, and ten minutes later Madison walks in.

"I'm sorry about my father. I had a long talk with him. He doesn't like the fact that we are still "friends" but I convinced him that we have to be for the sake of this company. That we just went out for drinks to talk about our next fiscal year. Oh, here. Take my ring and take yours off. We don't want daddy seeing this. This business has grown exponentially over this past year and I am not letting it go." Madison leaves my office. I take a moment and think deeply about what she has said. I don't want this to be destroyed because of him either.

∼

"How did we manage to not set up a date night for some months?"

Madison says laughing to herself in the mirror while she applies her makeup.

"I don't know." I yell from our room looking for a tie that'll match my suit, "But I'm glad we finally are going out to eat. We need to enjoy the fruits of our labor. And our money." I go under the bed to find my black shoes I always wear to fancy places. As I search for the shoes, I see the letter under the bed. It has been a while since our secret Hawaii honeymoon. I open the letter and it's a note with documents of Madison stealing money from different businesses she is a partner of. There were an alleged five businesses whose money had mysteriously been moved around. And they were her clients. "Am I the sixth?" I think out loud. I didn't have a clue who sent this to me, there was no return address. But I am going to find out. I tie my shoes with purpose and quickly walk into Madison's makeup room where she is applying the last of her face.

"How do I look?" She asks turning to me with a smile. I don't smile back.

"Madison, I found this letter a month ago and didn't have a chance to look at it until now. Are these things true and please don't lie to me?" Madison walks over to look at the papers. She looks shocked after scanning the documents that were in the package. She looks at me but doesn't respond. "So you are not going to say anything?" I continue to press.

"What is there to say? I won't lie to you. This is true but baby I won't do that to you if that is what you're thinking. You are my husband." She drops the papers on her chair still looking at me. "Stealing from you is like stealing from me. And no one steals from Madison Wilson." She tries to kiss me but I back away. Taken aback she looks like she's about to lose her temper but she takes another second then her face softens. "So, you don't want me anymore, Doyle? I will never steal from you."

I can't answer her. I feel so betrayed and I don't want to say anything I'd regret so I walk out and she follows, yelling, "No one turns away Madison Wilson!" She grabs my arm and I turn around.

"You have to give me some time to digest what I just learned about you. I just found out that my wife, my business partner, is a thief. A con artist. We're professionals!"

"You're right. We are professionals. I will not take from you. We are in this together. I told you I wouldn't ever let you stray from me. Now it's your turn to tell me you will not let me stray from you." Madison begins to tear, but she holds back her tears since she doesn't like to cry. She believes it's a weakness. "I love who you are. And I know you still love who I am." She walks towards me and kisses me on the lips and I can't help but return it.

"You are right. We both love power." Then I start to realize I don't only love Madison, I'm addicted to her. There was a knock at the door. We both exchange stares but I was the one who went to open the door. It was Mr. Wilson.

∽

It's been a while since I saw Madison. She won't return any of my phone calls or emails. I don't know how she is doing her work at D n' M but she is putting in her hours. I told myself that after work I will go to her parents' house no matter what the cost. I deserve an answer. I went there not expecting her mother to answer the door but I'm glad she did. She advised me to wait outside and that Madison would come to the door shortly. When she came to the door she looked better than I was, considering we both haven't seen each other in a long time.

"So you don't return my calls or emails. I have no idea how you're doing besides the hours you have been putting in the books. I was drinking the other day thinking of you until I passed out. You said you wouldn't let me stray far from you… I miss your presence around me. I haven't been doing too well since you left the house. Can you come back home?"

"I can't." Madison closes the door behind her. "My father said I will lose my inheritance and my percent of the will if I don't leave you." Madison held back her tears. Unlike the last time we were together, they were really coming down this time. "Here's my ring. You can pawn it."

"That's it? Just like that. You're leaving me? What about our business? Our plans? This marriage?" I felt my eyes stinging red from the tears, little burning waterfalls were going down my cheeks.

She whispered sharply to me, regaining a bit of her composure, "Doyle, stop the crying. Don't show weakness. We will still have the business together. We just won't be married. I need my inheritance and my place in the will. I'm sorry. But we will still see each other at the office." Madison's mom called her from inside the house. "I got to go. Take care. See you at work. I will come back at the beginning of the week. Go get a drink, it will help you deal with this situation. Bye."

So I did just that for the rest of the weekend, just to get to Monday quicker.

∼

It's been another year and my business continued to be everything I dreamed it would. Another year older with all work, no play. I decided to take a trip to Maine to buy their famous lobsters. My trip was very uneventful without anyone to share it with. Madison and I were still sneaking around and it would've been too suspicious for both of us to take a vacation at the same time. I stopped by a nearby liquor store before heading inside the hotel. I unpacked my suitcase and laid down on the bed. I pulled out the bottle and chugged away. As I was halfway done with the bottle, I saw that it was about 5 o'clock and I remembered the lobsters. I was hungry and it was my reason for being in Maine after all, so I closed the door behind me and bumped into Antoinette.

"Oh my..." I was fixing my clothes, Anna always made me get that way. "There is no way I thought I would see you again."

"Yes, way. Now look at you looking fly for sure. Now what are you doing in Maine?" She asked giving me a hug. I didn't know how much of her touch I was missing.

"I'm on vacation and I wanted to come here for the lobsters. I heard it was good. Do you care to come with?" Anna laughed and said, of course, she already knew a great place for us to go eat.

We both enjoyed our time together. The food was amazing, everything that I could ever want in one sitting. Lobster, whole crab, shrimp scampi, garlic shrimps, corn on the cob, and big baked potatoes. I missed talking to her. She looked so different, still beautiful but matured. Not in age but in experience and energy. She told me that she'd be moving soon but now it was permanent. She saved enough money to go to school and finally become a teacher. I was very happy to hear that. After we talked and walked to our hotel, I invited her up to my room. I didn't expect to have a nightcap like the one we had that night. The sexual chemistry was strong between us and we enjoyed every bit of each other. I didn't know how much we missed each other until we made our sweet music.

I woke up the next day from the most peaceful sleep I've had in a long time and felt something I hadn't felt before. I couldn't describe what it was but it felt warm and relaxing. I looked over at Anna who was stirring awake.

"Were you watching me sleep?" She said with an enchanting smile.

"Yes, I was. And you are beautiful to me." I kissed her forehead.

"I still love you, Doyle."

"I still love you, Anna Thomas." She chuckled as I gently poked her nose.

We made morning love in the shower and after we got dressed she gave me a tour of Maine since she had been there a month before me. Maine is very appealing. We bought a pizza from a nearby restaurant and brought it to the hotel after our tour. We had so much to converse about over the years. I asked her if she dated anyone since we stopped talking and she mentioned that she tried but traveling made things complicated. She asked me about Madison, and I told her how we got married, her thievery, and the divorce.

"Things will get better and you will find someone who will love you for you."

"I think I am staring at her." Anna's face flushed. Then I kissed her cheek. "I know you are the one."

∼

"I now pronounce you husband and wife. You may kiss your bride."

I kiss Antoinette's beautiful face and lift her up in the air. Embracing her she tells me that I just made her the happiest woman in the world. I kiss her again and walk down the aisle hand and hand to our family throwing rice and petals at us. After the reception, we went straight to the airport for our honeymoon to Jamaica. The water was beautiful and the air was clean but I felt troubles coming my way. I was trying really hard not to break, but with everything, the wedding, the business, Antoinette, and Madison, anguish came to me in waves. Anna sees it and questions my health. I tell her we have to go back to the hotel when we were just about to book the Jet Ski.

I sit her down and began to speak rivers. The real problem is that I can't live a day without drinking whiskey and it had been two days with getting ready for the vacation as well as the preparations for the wedding. "I become agitated and angry. Madison thought it would be a way to help me deal with life…But then she left me. And now I'm with you and I can't stop drinking. I shouldn't be feeling angry now. I would be lying to you if I said I didn't miss Madison. But I love you. I'm so confused." She removes herself from my embrace and stands up. I take her cue and stand up in front of her and she doesn't veer from my eyes. Silently, she begins to weep.

I sigh but I'm sure she notices I'm agitated. "Don't cry. That's a weakness."

"This. Is. Not. Weakness. Doyle." She wipes her tears. "This is what strength looks like. You can cry and be strong. I have emotions and I am using them to express how I feel." She looks at me and slaps me really hard. "You've hurt me. Out of all days." Anna walks into the kitchen to pour wine in a glass. I walk behind her to fight for this. The last thing I need is for her to leave me like Madison.

"Baby, I don't know what is right or wrong anymore. Madison believes showing sadness is a weakness. Madison says I can have everything I want if I am in control!"

"Madison. Madison. Madison. This is all I am hearing from you." Anna takes a sip of her wine and walks towards me on the other side of the counter.

"What do you want? Madison has you so far gone, you don't even remember when she took your feet and made them her own…Baby, Madison didn't mean you any good." She says caressing my face. "I can help you. I can show you how to be a man and be in control of your emotions and life." Anna kisses me. "But not with Madison still in your head telling you what to do."

"I love you Anna. I'm coming to the realization that I love Madison's energy. I was turned on by her power and control. That is not the type of love I want…Please help me though, I don't know what to do."

"Thank you for realizing this. This is the first step to getting better." She stares into my eyes. "If we have a child, I don't want him to know anything about your drinking problems or Madison. I will stay with you for however long is forever. My father used to beat on my mother when he got angry because he couldn't drink. Don't do the same to me."

"Never will I be your father and Madison is no more. We will have a son, and I will show him how to be a man." Anna laughs because she once told me she wanted to have a girl. I, on the other hand, want a son so he can run my business.

~

I love this new life that I have with Antoinette and she is such an amazing person. She loves her teaching job and seems to be even happier since we found out she was pregnant. I'm so happy for us but I am always at work and I found that it is very hard for me to support Anna the way she needs me to support her. I try my best but the strain of the pregnancy can sometimes weigh heavy on us both.

As I walk into my home I can't believe my eyes. On my couch I find a man caressing and kissing my wife's belly as he kneels between my wife's legs. Without even closing the door I lunge at him, tackling him to the ground. I introduce his eyes to my fist as I slam his head through our glass table. I can control my emotions for most things but disrespect is not one of them. I still demand control of what's mine.

"What are you doing?!" Anna screamed at me as she pushes me away just as I was about to throw him through the entertainment center. "I called you several times because I needed you to get home to help me. I was in pain and you didn't call me back." She walks over to the man who is trying to get up. Anna asks if he is okay, and embraces the part of his head that went through the table.

"I don't like the way you are touching him right now." I start walking to Anna who is ignoring me.

"Are you alright?"

"Yes. I'm okay." He says while watching me.

"This is Franco Sanchez. He works at the company I used to work for. He wants to be a teacher as well. He transferred over here recently and called me. I was in the middle of needing someone to help me get through the pain. The baby was kicking me, it hurt so badly. That's why I called you but you didn't answer your phone. Franco called when I needed help and offered to come over to help ease my pain. He was just rubbing my stomach and talking to the baby...It worked." Anna glares at me sharply.

"Baby I'm sorry. My secretary gave Madison my calls when she left today and I was in meetings all day." I look at this bastard touching my woman. "But he shouldn't be touching you! If you were in that much pain you should have gone to the hospital. If I see you touching my woman again-"

"No Doyle. I couldn't move. Don't blame Franco for helping me when I needed you. You know the condition that I'm in." Anna says as she helps Franco to his feet. "Madison knew I needed you and didn't bother to tell you. Madison believes in herself, not family. I warned you about her. You won't ever get it." Anna says walking towards the door. "Thank you for coming to see me Franco. Let me know where you end up and when you become a teacher. I'll make sure to visit."

"Sure." Franco says walking towards the door. He stops to look at me then back at Anna. "I'm going to live in Wilmington. The best schools for teaching. I'll see to it that you visit me, alright?" Franco gives Anna a hug. "Take care of this girl. Or someone else will."

"Are you in love with Franco?"

"Look, baby. Things happen. We were on bad terms and when we split up I thought we weren't going to be together anymore."

"You hurt me really bad, you know? You think Madison and I are messing around behind your back, so you seek revenge, and got pregnant."

"No, this is your baby. This is not Franco's." Anna says to me as she walks down the stairs behind me."

Jahem please go upstairs baby, and let me and daddy talk down here, okay? I'll come up and get you when I am done. We can go to the park and get ice cream, okay?"

"Mom." Jahem says to his mother annoyed. "It's the summertime. The rec center field is open. Can I play soccer after you and dad finish talking?"

"Yes." Anna tolls Jahem as he runs upstairs. Anna walks towards me. "Baby, it's obvious we need more time away from each other. As Jahem said, it's the summertime. So I'll visit my mom for a while and take Jahem with me."

"Is that child mine, Antoinette?" Anna looks at me and a single tear falls from her watery eyes.

"This child is yours, Doyle. Are you still screwing with Madison behind my back?" I walk over to Anna and grab her hands.

"I love you. I don't have room for any other woman. When I needed help, it was you who was there. I know I can always count on you."

∽

"Hello. Did you do what I told you to do?"

"Yes, Madison. I told her I loved her and that she's the only woman for me."

"Great. Now no matter what, you have to keep telling her, or else she will suspect something."

"I know what to tell her."

"Soon you will have the best of both worlds."

"Yes. I already have a life at home. Now I just need you and my business."

"Of course, I will always be here. Daddy's dead. I got his will and my inheritance. Now I can finally be with you. Come over today. Let's drink to celebrate."

Chapter Six:

The Intent

Jahem

"Good morning. How was your day yesterday?" Mom asks as I sit down to eat.

"It was good mom. You give great advice, it really paid off." I hope I sound relaxed. My body was feeling so weird since last night. There is a heat coming from me that a cold shower couldn't fix "It was fun. I think she is starting to like me."

"That's great Jahem!" She says enthusiastically. "Just…don't put your guard down yet. You still have to respect Suesan and Colton's relationship.

"When we were on our date, she told me she didn't want to be with him. She told me a lot of things about him.

"Okay that may be honey but they're still together. What exactly did she tell you?" My mother stops messing with the toaster and looks at me.

"Just about his life. His family separated when he was two. His mom doesn't care about him much. His father was selfish and wanted everything for himself, so he isn't around much."

"Well Jahem, remain alert. Pity does not leave much room for the heart." She turns away from me and I made it clear to listen. "Just because someone feels sorry for a person it doesn't mean that's love."

She didn't turn back around. Instead, she takes a deep breath and looks out the kitchen window.

"It sounds like you know something about pity and love." I say to her, kind of prying. She doesn't respond. "Rest assured mom. I'm alert... I hear you."

"So what's for breakfast?" My father asks as he comes from upstairs. I woke up earlier than usual because he came home early this morning and he was bringing in boxes from his car. By now he has changed as well, now he was in a Hanes white t-shirt, his boxers, and flip-flops. I guess he wasn't going to work today.

"Your favorite honey, beef bacon and waffles with grits." My mom sounds her best in front of him. She's never the one to show him her tears and struggles.

"That sound all good right, son?" He asks me and pats my shoulder. We stare at one another for some time. Is he really that clueless? He's been gone for days and now he wants to come back and pick up where he left off? My mom clears her throat and she snaps me out of my trance.

I move over, allowing his hand to come down, "Yeah, actually mom, I am not really hungry. Okay?" I say moving away from him and my half-empty plate. My dad looks at me as if I just slapped him in his face. Then he looks back at mom.

"What's wrong with you?" He is asking with his fist on his waist as if he cares but he doesn't. He is even sitting there looking like the dads from the department store catalogs. He only cares about himself and his job with his ex. He tries to pretend so much, it's a shame he believes his own lies.

When I continue to walk away he reaches for me, grabbing my arm and for a second my blood circulation cuts off. I jerk back and yank my arm away from him. "Just leave me alone, Doyle!" When I used those words, I knew I shouldn't have.

"WHAT!?!" He slams his hand down on the kitchen table. "COME HERE RIGHT NOW BOY. FOR I BEAT YOU. DO YOU UNDERSTAND?!"

Here we go again. This isn't the first time he uses this to intimidate me. I lost respect for him a long time ago and I'm not backing down now.

"What Doyle?!" I say as I turn around to look at him.

"Don't call me that, I AM YOUR FATHER." He takes slow steps toward me and I meet his step with another step back. I trust him at the distance of a long devil's stick.

"All you care about are titles. And that's all you'll ever be to me. You should just go to hell already. Don't come back like everything is cool and expect us to be COOL." He stops in his tracks. "Doyle you can just KISS MY--"

"Jahem!!! That's no way to talk to your father." My mom says shaking her head behind his back with pleading eyes. "Now you need to apologize to him." With a silent breath, she says, "Please." I stay silent and just look at her. I don't believe how much she continues to cover for this guy.

"Whatever I did to you I am sorry but you are going to respect me. Do you understand, Jahem?" He says trying to level with me.

"You know what, you are right." I look at back at him. "You are sorry."

RiNg....rInG....riNG,

Before anyone can say another word the phone rang.

"Hello..." My mother quickly answers the phone. "Suesan..." She looks at me. "Okay here he is, nice talking to you, sweetie. Hold on." She walks to give me the phone and gestures for me to go upstairs. As I took the phone and jog up the stairs, I can hear my father still going on and on about the disrespect he feels in his own house.

"Hello Suesan." I say as calm and cool as I could but my body was still feeling this crazy heat on the inside. "How are you?"

"Good. I'm just calling to see how you're doing." She seems very nervous.

"I'm doing well. Hey, how'd you get my home phone number?"

"I got it from DJ, I hope you don't mind?"

"No. it's okay." I try to sound flattered and surprised but most of all, grateful. "Well, what's up?"

Wounds Remain

"I was wondering, do you want to go to the park with me? It's a nice day outside." She sounds very cute on the phone.

"Okay, I could be ready in two hours. When were you getting ready and planning to go? I wanted to do my homework."

"Two hours sound just about right."

"Okay, I'll pick you up."

As I hang up the phone, my mom calls me into the kitchen to talk about my father of all things. I didn't have anything to say to her about him but all my mom wants is for us to get along. That's not going to happen.

"Unless he stays here with us at home, doesn't go to that job, and he fires Madison, I don't think I can be friendly to him." The look on my mothers' face kills me but she has taught me to be honest with her. And I can't hold most things back from her. I need to change the conversation though, I have to see Suesan soon. "Ma, I'd love to sit and talk about this more but I'm driving to see Suesan, I'll be back later." I stand up to give my mother a hug.

"No you not." My father interjects walking back into the kitchen.

"Doyle, just let him go." My mom says holding on to me.

"No and that's final." My dad stomps upstairs to his room and slams the door.

"When I'm done with my homework, I'm going okay?"

"I know." She gives me another hug. "I'll handle your father."

I kiss my mother on the forehead and head upstairs. I sat on my bed thinking of ways I can save my mother from his lies and deceit. It is weighing on her and I hated it. But my mind keeps shifting to Suesan. I immediately start my homework while still wondering in the back of my mind how I can save both.

"History...15 questions on this page, six questions in chapter nine, and eight vocabulary words. Then our final class project."

I finish my work, shower, and call Suesan in an hour and forty-five minutes. I go downstairs to say bye to my mother.

"Hey mom." I say confidently as I walk into the living room.

"Look at you, all nice and fresh looking. She must be something else." Mom says playfully.

"Yeah" I pause to put on my shades. "Something like that."

"Well," mom giggles, "your father stepped out so get your motor going and leave before he gets back. And have fun." I give her one last hug. I love my mom a lot and I know how much I mean to her.

I call Suesan up on my cell and ask her to come outside when I'm walking to her front door. An unknown lady opens the door. She is tall but not taller than me, long hair, pretty, and well dressed.

"Hello Jahem. Suesan will be with you shortly, come in." The lady opens the door wide enough for me to walk through.

"I am Suesan's mother. You can call me Clarissa. And this here is her sister Mia." As she points to her daughter.

"Hello, I'm 12, are you here for my sister?"

"Yes, I am here for Suesan, we are going to hang out for a little bit."

"Okay, I'm ready." Suesan says.

I turn around to greet her and man does she take my breath away. There was a peach flower attached to a clip in her hair filled with her curls. She wore a matching green and peach halter-top and skirt. She sure can dress and looks like she thinks about every outfit.

"You look nice." Her mom says as she looks at me.

"Thank you." She smiles at her mom and looks at me. I couldn't feel my face but I think my silence said it all. "Let me just say bye to Luis and Mark." She goes over to say bye to her brothers and she was just angelic. "Oh mother, Gloria is asleep right now." Clarissa nods walking towards the door.

"Have fun." Clarissa says as we start to walk out.

"Nice to meet you, Ms. Clarissa. I hope to see you all again."

"You too Jahem." Clarissa and Mia add.

Walking to the car and opening the passenger door I tell Suesan, "Your family is nice."

We get to the park around 1:00 and that's when we discover one another's childish ways. I'm on the monkey bars. She is on the slides. We play on the tires and swings. I even teach her how to hang upside down. We play hide and seek around the trees and bushes. It's nice to see that we don't have to be like those stuffy couples. I really like that we could cut loose and show each other who we really are. Eventually, we were both getting hungry. Once we decided on Burger King we ordered through the drive-thru and sat in the car with our food.

"So was Miss Jordan's homework long or what?" Suesan says playfully while noshing on a fry.

"Yes… it was pretty long. But I didn't mind it, I know it's all worth it." I say looking at her as she eats her fries. Those lips. The memories.

"Yeah, that's the positive side to it. I don't mind it, it's just like a test. But I would've rather taken a test." There is a sudden pause in her voice. Her face becomes serious. "Jahem, I like you a lot. There's something about you that's starting to make me feel different about myself. In a good way and I am relaxed around you." She looks up at me. "You give me everything that I need. I know this is only the second time we spent time together but you give me enough to want to know more about you, and… I am not ready to let this go." Suesan shakes her head and looks out the window.

"Suesan…I feel the same way." I slowly reach for her hand. She turns to look at me. "I've been waiting to hear that." I caress her face, while I reach over to kiss her lips. There's always something in the pit of my stomach when it knows what I am doing is wrong. I pull away and state the one thing I do not want to hear myself say. "Suesan, we can't do this. We are both falling head over heels in love but you have a boyfriend. You know he won't let us forget."

"I know but this right here feels good." She says with a longing look in her eyes and she grabs my hands. "And I know the difference between a great guy and a guy who uses me. And you are not Colton and that is all that matters to me…" She slowly touches my lips and I close my eyes to feel her hands caressing my face. "As far as I'm concerned I want you and not him."

I don't want to disappoint her but I know this will not end well. Colton is going to be pissed. Suesan is shaking and I can tell she longs for me the way I long for her. I give her a hug and kiss her temple. I whisper, "I won't ever let you go. You got me. Forever." She thanks me but at what cost will our selfishness have us pay?

I parked my car in the back of the house and sat on the couch and watched B.E.T. My mom came downstairs and sat next to me with glasses on.

"Hey, Mom…" I turn to her. "What's with the shades, Stevie Wonder? I say playing around. I didn't realize until she wasn't laughing that something happened and I questioned her again more concerned.

"No, baby that's fine. Everything is okay." She said softly as she rested her head back on the couch.

I removed the glasses off her face and could not believe what I saw. My father had hit my mom. Her face was bruised on the left, and her right eye was closed. What would tempt this animal to hit her? And with a rush of blood to my head, it dawns on me that I DID THIS.

"Mom…" I grabbed her hand. "I'm so, so sorry."

"I fought back and bruised his face." She stared towards the kitchen. "He tried to push me down the stairs and I dug my nails into his arms. I knocked my head against the wall as I fell backward when he shook me off. He chased me into the kitchen when he saw I was able to get up from the floor. He fell to the ground trying to catch up to me. I took the vase that grandma gave me and hit him before he could get up. I think he was unconscious." She started to cry. "I didn't know what to do. I dragged him outside while only seeing him with one eye. I took his keys and locked all the doors." The good eye widened as big as a saucer. "Was he still out there in the front?" Her lips started to quiver and fresh tears fell down her cheek.

"I came in through the back." I got up to check the front window. I picked up my phone from the couch and proceeded to call the cops. It didn't look like she had the chance to, nor did I think she would have on her own. She looked very bad but she's tough. "Seventeen West Gray St. between Prairie and Hill Avenue. I would like to report a domestic violence situation. It's my mother… 10 minutes…. I'll stay on the phone… Thank you."

I cleaned up the smashed vase on the floor and left the house the way it was until the police arrived. I led them to my mom and they filed a report, took pictures of her face, her back and every room in the house where the incident happened. One police officer came down with two liquor bottles. They were in my mom's room and the police said he was drunk when he had hit her. I could have told them that. I wanted to press charges and I told the police. Surprisingly, my mother agreed. They took down his known associates, relatives and anyone that could be hiding him, including his job address and his ex-wife.

I took mom upstairs with the help of another police officer. The police officer and I laid my mother down slowly on her bed. I wiped her eyes and she fell asleep. They left soon after and reassured us they were coming back tomorrow. I walked the officers to the door and one of them gave me his card to call him directly. I put the card up in my room, took a shower, ironed my clothes, and got into bed, but could not sleep.

I wake up to my phone alarm. It's Monday. I think I'll skip school today and take care of mom. There were some other things I just thought of that needed to get done. After I brush my teeth I call Home Depot and talk to their locksmiths to see about changing all of our outside locks. Then I go to my mom's room to see if she's okay. She's fast asleep so I decide to be the one to make her breakfast for a change. Pancakes, bacon, eggs, and freshly squeezed orange juice. When it's all done, I take the platter up to her with the morning newspaper.

"Hello mother." I greet her as I place her breakfast and newspaper on the bed. I walk over to pull the curtains back to allow some sun to shine through. She is already stirring awake. "How are you feeling? I'm not going to school today so I can take care of you and get some things done around the house." I say this as I sit on the edge of the bed, allowing her some space. My mom nods her head in approval. I advise my mother not to speak, seeing what the fight between her and that damn animal caused her. I am blessed that she can still operate in some ways on her own. Overnight her face got a bit puffier.

After we eat I help her into the wheelchair I got from the basement. Eventually, after reading her newspaper and being idle for too long, she wants to go downstairs. First I take down the wheelchair, then I help mom, taking one step at a time to help her down the stairs. As I got down the stairs I turn the TV on to her favorite channel, Comedy Central. She could use some laughs. I gave her the remote as I go into the kitchen to clean.

I call my mom's primary doctor for help. In this situation, he agrees to make a house call. In the meantime, I give her a heating pad for her back, legs, and neck. I hope the warmth will soothe her. I hear a car pull up near my house. I look outside. It was the people here to fix the locks. I tell them where every door was in the house. They take all of 30 minutes and as they left there were DJ and Suesan approaching the door. Not a good time. But I smile nevertheless.

"What's up Jahem?" DJ says.

"Hey Jahem. Why were you not in school?" Suesan asks.

"Come in, I'm not going to be in school for a while y'all because my mom got into a fight with my father." As I motion them in.

"Hello Mrs. Thomas." Suesan says with sympathy.

"I advise for both of them to leave, Jahem. I really don't need the extra help. I'm fine kids, it's already a busy day." My mom says hurting. They understand and see them out. The doctor is coming out of his car as my friends walk away. It has been a long day.

He starts by examining her bruising and swelling. He gives me a prescription for painkillers. He also mentions that he'll be checking on her periodically for a couple of weeks. When he leaves I drive to the pharmacy to put the prescription in. When I get back home we set up the living room space for her. I never left her side as I rested on the other couch. The police officer that gave me his card called me and said that there was a court date set for next month. We fell asleep watching B.E.T.

Wounds Remain

They fuck you up, your mom and dad. They may not mean to, but they do. They fill you with the faults they had and add some extra, just for you.

-Philip Larkin

Chapter Seven:

The Unforgettable

Jahem

I continued being upset that I couldn't do anything for my mom. Every time my father got drunk, he decides to beat on her. Maybe if I stood up to him more, he wouldn't hit her. When I checked on her this morning I noticed that the swelling that formed around her cheeks was no longer visible, and the bruises on her face and back were starting to lighten up into her former complexion. I hadn't seen that sandbag in a month. Since my school is close to home, every day during lunch, study hours, and after school, I had been leaving, rushing home to be with my mom. She was getting better and had her mobility. I was doing this more to make sure that he wasn't there. My mother told me to never rest the burdens of the world on my shoulders and it made it easier that DJ and Suesan helped the best way they could.

My mom is capable of moving now but I keep her wheelchair around. It's more for my sanity than her use when I'm at school. DJ and Suesan have been helping me around the house as well with the laundry, cooking, cleaning, and shopping errands. As for today, I had to go to football and basketball tryouts and I needed Suesan to watch her since DJ and I would be at tryouts. She agreed.

As usual, Suesan and I are still dating and our bond continues to grow in the absence of Colton. Colton and his anger got him in trouble and now he and everyone except the three brothers are in jail for fighting in a bar. He had a previous record and now facing this situation he's going to be spending some time in jail. Suesan hadn't seen him and I wasn't forcing her to, that's just fine with me. Her birthday was coming up and I want to put some focus on that, too. I have been in jewelry stores, shoe stores, and the stores in the mall that we went to on a few of our dates but I just don't know what to get her.

~

I left the instructions on the table but Suesan told me that she already knew what to do. This was true but it just made me feel better. I kissed her, said bye to mom, and left. I arrived at school and changed my clothes for basketball. Coach K made us do stretches, suicides, several drills, and a conditioning exercise. Finally, he split us into two teams and we had to play a pickup game. I scored 15 points and DJ scored 12. The coach said that he'd post the cuts for the next school year. I left and walked onto the field to join the rest for the football tryouts.

Coach Bullock told us to line up and he counted us off in groups. Two groups of eleven for defense and offense and then we rotated. Honestly, I did well on the defensive side but I was getting tired by the time we switched to offense. I'll see when Coach Bullock posts the cuts for the August preseason games.

I knocked on the back door to the house and Suesan opened up. There's a look Suesan gives me when something is on her mind and it's very short from being a good look. She said it quickly, "Your mother is in the hospital…" Nothing she said after that had registered. The world stopped and the only thing I could feel was my heartbeat. "Jahem, Jahem…" Suesan touched my hands. "We have to go now, they left with her a minute ago." I looked at Suesan and walked away. DJ just got to the house and Suesan caught him up as we got in the car. We all rushed into the emergency room looking for my mother.

I addressed the nurse at the front desk while trying to get rid of this lump in my throat. "Hi. I'm looking for my mother, Antoinette Thomas."

"Only close relatives can see Ms. Thomas."

The doctor said from behind us. I looked at DJ and Suesan and they both nodded for me to go. I opened the door and saw my mom laying in the bed with tubes and an i.v line in her.

I called her but she didn't respond. I slowly walked to her and grabbed her hand. The doctor followed me into the room and gave me some time with my mom but I didn't need it. I just wanted to know what was wrong. "There was no physical trauma or malady. Her vitals are stable, her blood samples came back okay. Judging on what has been going on according to your lady friend, your mother is suffering from chronic stress. High amounts of stress can do a lot of harm to the body, it also lowers immune function. Chronic stress disrupted your mother's ability to heal, making her body vulnerable to infections." He walked to me and put his hand on my shoulder. "The good news is your mother will be fine. She will stay here for a while and will be back home before you know it. For now, let her rest." I shook the doctor's hand off my shoulder and stood up to look at him.

"That's what she was doing before she arrived here. Anything else you recommend, Doc?" Was he assuming I wasn't helping her enough at home? I just stood looking at him for a second and then I realized it might've been a bit much. A bit more angry than embarrassed, I walked away, I can't possibly blame him for doing his job. He turned around before I opened the door. "Jahem, we will take good care of your mother. You've done well up to this point." I stopped for a second as if to say thank you. But then I kept walking.

Suesan and Doren looked at me when I got to the waiting room but I couldn't look back. The rage for my father was growing with every step. "She's staying the night but she's stable. Let's go." I was walking faster than normal and I heard them pacing behind me as they were trying to keep up. On the way back I decided to drop them off home. The car ride was quiet, just the sounds of the music breaking the tension.

"Bye. See you later man, I wish you good luck." Doren said as he gets out to give Suesan a hug and pounds my fist.

"Alright." I say still not looking at him, but instead straight ahead.

On the way to Suesan's house, she expressed she didn't want to go home but I couldn't stay with her. She gave me a kiss and took one last look at me before she left the car. I didn't turn to her until she left the car to walk towards her door. I had to make sure she at least got in safe. Now back to this place I called home to try and sleep.

∼

When I got home I called the town hospital to speak to the doctor who was assigned to my mother. She assured me that she was still stable and comfortable. I went into the kitchen to warm the food Suesan made for my mother. I sat down on the couch and drifted off to sleep after dinner. I woke up to a loud knocking at the door.

Besides the pounding, everything seems quiet and cold, yet I wasn't alone. I rubbed my eyes and went to open the door. When I opened it, there was a boy looking up at me with a handful of papers asking for Antoinette Thomas.

"She's not here right now." I said looking around to see who placed him here. "I'm her son. How can I help you?"

"Do...Do you know when she will be back?" The little boy asked looking passed me into the house.

"No." I said sharply. "Who dropped you off?" Still looking outside for anyone who might have circled around the block. He just kept scraping the front of his sneaker on the concrete step. "Are they coming back? Is anyone coming to get you?" I tried to press him but he didn't say a word, just shook his head no. In the midst of my troubles, I invited him in. It just felt wrong to leave him out there alone in the dark. I of all people know how it feels. "Come in and sit on the couch."

I wondered what he wanted with my mother. I looked at the clock that read 8:45. Then I looked back at him. What am I going to do with him? I can't help but look him up and down. He's definitely scared but I need to know what his deal is so I can help him. I tell him to wait on the couch while I go to my room. I tried to find a blanket that wasn't too big for him. "This will do," I thought. "You can put this around you and sleep on the couch for tonight. But tomorrow you will have to talk to me." I brought down some more sheets and a pillowcase. I couldn't tell if he was hungry but I fixed him a pb&j sandwich. I took a shower as he ate the sandwich. Until I know more tomorrow, he is not leaving my sight. So I laid on the other couch and tossed and turned all night. He slept soundly.

I woke up the next morning with this little boy still asleep. The papers he was holding onto the night before had now fallen on the floor. I bent over to pick them up and as if my life couldn't get more bizarre, the documents said that my mother, Ms. Thomas, was Jaramia Sanchez's mother. My heart dropped. A birth certificate? This can't be right. This makes him 10. I was 6 when he was born. I continue to read, Ms. Thomas is the legal guardian of Jaramia Sanchez. My body suddenly felt heavy while my head felt light. I couldn't do anything but drop on the floor and stare at this little boy who just crashed into my life and I can almost make out a familiar face.

"Where's my mommy?" Jaramia asked sadly, as he rubbed his eyes looking right at me.

"Jaramia..." I paused at the sound of his name, "she will be here... Don't worry."

I slowly collected myself and went into the kitchen to fix him something to eat and I tell him he can follow me. When he finally looked at me I saw that Jaramia was lighter than me with curls. He had my mother's eyes, lips, my mother's everything. I ran a bath for him and told him to go play in the tub for a while. I set him up with some fresh clothes that I found in his book-bag. I stared at him when he came into the living room, he also resembled me. We are different but the same. I needed answers.

"So who gave you those papers?" I was very determined. He just looked at me like I was speaking a different language. "Um, I know your name is Jaramia, but I don't know how you got here. Do you know who brought you to my mother?" He quickly stared at me when I mention my mother but didn't say anything. He seemed very interested in my keys that I had left on the table last night. I looked at my keys then I looked at him. "Do you want to take a ride?" I asked. He smiled and I took that as a yes.

∼

I parked the car at the back of the lot, it gave us more time to walk and talk. "So... Jaramia, my name is Jahem do you like going to the mall?" Nothing. "Um, do you need new clothes?" Still nothing. He kept on looking straight, gripping onto his papers like someone was going to take them. Then my phone rang. It was DJ telling me he went by my house today and he and Suesan were worried about me. If only they knew, right?

"I'm fine." I reassured him. "But I'm a little busy right now."

"Alright man," DJ said with uncertainty. "Suesan and I will pass by your crib a little later."

When we got inside, it looked like he had never been in the mall before. He was a little resistant at first, at all of the noise and the size of the stores but he warmed up to the idea of walking in the mall. He fixed his eyes on the kid play area and I told him if I can buy him some clothes that we can come back and I promised. He did not say yes but he nodded in agreement.

It was not long until we finished and the kiddie center wasn't the only thing on his mind. I was getting hungry too as he pointed to the food court. I had him guide me to what he wanted. His choice was McDonald's. I didn't like it but I was cutting the kid a break. He was still quiet but I was glad he could count. He used his fingers to tell the cashier his food of choice and then I found a small table where we could eat. I put the bags on one chair and we sat on the other two. He had an appetite but I could see that he was still nervous. And he ate slowly like my mother, too. He didn't sit straight up in the chair just like a cousin I know.

We arrived in front of the building where the kiddy center was. I put the bags down and paid for an hour worth of rides. It seemed like he was having fun but I could feel his troubles.

~

We made it home at 2:00. I brought Jaramia into the house and I sat him in the living room and turned the television on. He seemed pleased. I cleaned the living room and the dining room while he was occupied then I started to cook shortly after. After that lunch I was interested in some home cooked fried chicken and yellow rice from the box. I was really missing mom. In the middle of cooking I called the hospital. They told me that they were doing tests and I'd have to call them later, but everything was in order for her to be released soon. That's when I started to worry. After I recollected myself, I headed into the living room to check on Jaramia. He was glued to the television. I called Suesan during the last and final turns of the chicken.

"Hey sweetheart. How is it going?"

"Hello, Jahem." She exhaled deeply. "I was worried about you."

"I know, Doren was texting me. I'm alright. I'll talk to you tomorrow, love. I just wanted to check in."

"Talk to you tomorrow, babe."

After dinner, I had left Jaramia playing in the living room and did my homework at the kitchen table. While working on some of my projects he came into the kitchen. "Jaramia, I thought I put you to bed?"

"Is this mommy?" He was holding a picture he took from my room. I took it from him and stared at it. I got to pay better attention to him.

"Yes, Jaramia... that's..." I felt my throat closing up with every breath I took. I couldn't deny anymore. "That's our mother." I finally say it out loud. "Come sit." Gesturing him over, I was excited that he spoke for the first time and in some weird way, it was like I was waiting for him to accept me the whole time. "Everything will be okay, Jaramia." I stared at the picture again as he slowly drifted back into his sleep. I put him on my chest and he fell soundly asleep. I got the papers that Jaramia was holding onto so dearly. Do I even want to continue reading?

It says that he was born here in Wilmington. My mother...Did. Not. Cheat. On. Him. I pushed those words out from my lips as the tears flowed quickly from my eyes that I tried to inhale back in. As I turned the pages they revealed to me that he'd been changed from one foster parent to another, twice since his father died two years ago. He ran away from one of them. As I flip to the next crumbled paper, attached to another birth certificate, it says the father's name was Franco Sanchez. No relatives in Wilmington but a known relative in...

Allentown? I look at the pictures of when he was born, I recognize one the pictures and it was of my mom when she was younger. Other pictures I guess were of Franco and Jaramia when he was little. I didn't want to read these anymore. I slowly let the papers fall from my hands. I stared at the rain outside as Jaramia snored on me.

I woke up to crows chirping in a yellow and blue sky. I felt drained, lonely, and helpless for Jaramia. This was all too much to take in. Our mom was in the hospital and she must have cheated on her husband. The husband who beats and cheats on her. I don't blame her. And I'm so in love with Suesan but I'm in a similar situation. Am I any better than Doyle? And Jaramia, my little brother, I couldn't help but feel like there was more pain awaiting this family and we were just prisoners to time.

I woke Jaramia up and told him to get in the tub. I helped him wash his hair because he didn't do such a good job before. There was a knock at the door.

"Finish up Jaramia. Your clothes are right there. I will be back." I told him as I started to walk towards the door. "I wonder who this could be."

"It's Suesan." She said ecstatically.

"Oh…hi." Looking back towards the bathroom, "Suesan what's going on. How are you? Come in." I greeted her as I slowly moved away from the entrance.

"Thank you." She replied as I took her coat. "I just had to come and see if everything was okay over here."

"Everything's fine." I gestured around trying to block her from wanting to go to the bathroom. "Listen, it's a bad t-"

"Mommy." Jaramia said poking his head out of the bathroom.

"Jaramia, I told you I'd be right back." I said nervously.

"Who is this, Jahem?" Suesan asked walking towards Jaramia. She bent down in front of him.

"He is my younger brother. Suesan, meet Jaramia." I stated as I closed the door.

She seemed confused but she's great with kids. "Hello Jaramia, my name is Suesan, nice to meet you." Suesan held out her hand but he was too shy to shake it.

"I won't hurt you, Jaramia." Suesan assured him, "I'm Jahem's friend."

"He'll warm up to you, just give him some time." I picked him up to comfort him. "Jaramia came knocking at my door yesterday. Go read those papers over there on the table. Her expressions varied from concentrated to curious to heartfelt to worried. She returned back to me while I was in the kitchen. By this point, he was playing with his hot wheels on the entertainment center. "I had asked him about where he came from yesterday but he didn't respond much. So I just stopped trying and I thought that if the hospital said my mother can have visitors that I might let him see our mother.

"I don't know if you should worry your mother at the hospital. And what about school, or have you forgot?" She asked curiously.

"It's tough but I have that under control. He will stay here and I'll visit him during my lunch and prep time. I'll come straight home after school. What else am I going to do? I have to step up…just until mom gets out and we can work out how he's going to go to school and stuff. He is my brother and I have a bigger responsibility now." I looked at him. "More than ever. Plus, I will just get the homework and assignments whenever I can.

"Look Jahem, the school kind of already knows what's going on. I will get you the homework and class assignments, and that should give you a few more days. Don't worry about that. We're in this together." I walked over to Suesan with appreciation in my eyes and love in my heart and hugged her. I admire her.

"Thank you Suesan and that's why you are so special to me.

∼

We all were watching TV in the living room. Talking, laughing and having a great time. Although Jaramia is laughing he is still holding onto me tight, then Suesan had a suggestion, "Jahem let's put something on that Jaramia will like to see." I'm sure she was doing this so he'd be more comfortable.

"Yeah sure, why not? Do you want to watch Spiderman or Rugrats, Jaramia?"

"Spiderman." He gestured by using a pretend web shooter with his right hand.

"Spiderman it is." I put it on DisneyXD and they were still showing commercials. "Jaramia, can you help me get us some snacks in the kitchen?" He nodded his head yes and obediently followed me.

"Um, GRAPE." Jaramia said as I placed two drinks in front of him. "I like Suesan, she's funny." He said looking back at her smiling." I was amazed as to how much he was talking right now. I looked at him and admired him for his progress.

"Yeah Suesan is something else." I gazed over at her. "I like her too." I told him as I turned to reach in the cabinet for chips, cookies and the last handful of grapes. We headed back into the living, where the cartoon was just beginning. I gave Suesan her drink as I sat down and when Suesan was getting ready to kiss me as she said thank you, Jaramia plopped right between us. We both looked at each other and started to laugh.

"Shh." Jaramia said as we both apologized in a whisper.

Later that evening Doren showed up, "Hey Bro, come in what's going on?" I asked as I gave him a hug.

"Nothing much. Just wanted to check in..." Doren paused and looked at Jaramia. "And who is this little fella?" Doren asked quizzically.

"DJ, this is my little brother, Jaramia."

"Jaramia this is my best friend Doren but you can call him DJ if you like." I told Jaramia as I winked at him.

"He does look like you and your mother but not Doyle though." Doren observed as he sat down on the couch.

"Um... he's not Doyle's..."

"So, your mother cheated." Doren concluded as Suesan hit him in the leg. "Ouch." Doren said as he rubbed his leg. "Alright bro, I did not mean anything by it." DJ announced apologetically. "It's just a pretty big surprise. I'm sorry."

"Don't think nothing of it, I'm just annoyed, that is all. Grab a snack."

"So..." DJ looks at me then at Jaramia. "Jaramia, hi. I am DJ."

"He's not going to say anything to you."

"Why?" He wondered.

"If you come back tomorrow and spend time with him, he will talk to you."

"Okay well, what y'all getting ready to do?" He asked sitting up in the chair.

"I am about to put him to bed then I'm chilling with y'all for a little while. You staying a little longer Suesan?"

"Yeah I guess." She said tiredly as she got up from the floor and lied on the couch that Jaramia just stood up from.

"Alright, I will be right back." I pick up Jaramia and took him in my room, so he could get some sleep. "Look, Jaramia can you go to sleep up here while I am just downstairs with my friends?"

"I will try but can you leave the door open? I am afraid of the dark."

"Sure, I will do that, just give me a call if you need anything but just try to get some sleep okay?"

"Okay, Jahem. Thank you. Love you." Yawning his way to sleep I gave him a kiss on the head. I closed the door slightly and took one more look at him before I left.

"So what is going on here with y'all?" I asked Suesan and DJ when I get downstairs.

"Nothing really, Jahem. We were just talking about that time when you tried to show off your new car."

"Haha, yeah, I felt cool then, still do now that you both are kickin' it with me. But looking back it was really funny though."

"Funny, Jahem that was hilarious." DJ pointed out.

"Okay, okay anyway do you all want something to drink?" I said smirking at both of them.

"I do." said Suesan. DJ just gave me a thumbs up.

I returned with their drinks to see DJ sitting awfully close to Suesan whispering in her ear. I wanted to see the next move they were going to make but DJ started to tickle her in places I should only touch.

"What are ya'll doing in here?" I said seriously.

"Oh nothing, DJ was just trying to cheer me up because I had some problems at school ever since Colton went to jail.

I looked back and forth at the both of them and DJ was a mind reader because one cold look from me and he moved far from Suesan. I sat next to Suesan and handed them both their drinks. I asked Suesan why she's going to DJ about problems she is having instead of me.

"Baby." Suesan put her drink on the table to grab my hands. "You are going through a lot with your mom, dad, and now your brother. I didn't want to add to your stress. You aren't at school and seeing how we all have become close I thought DJ can help defend me. You know my situation sweetheart."

"It doesn't matter Suesan you can come to me about anything, regardless." I looked toward DJ who was now sitting in the lounge chair across from us. "And you my bro, you should have told me what the deal was at school. I might not be there much these days but I am there. It was wrong for the both of you to keep this from me. You know how I feel about her." I looked at Suesan, "especially you."

"We won't ever do that again. We are all in this together." Suesan said with sincerity.

"Bro, don't worry. I was watching out for your girl, while you figure things out over here. We straight, there's nothing going on." DJ patted me on the back. "Now if you don't mind, I am going to stay the night and rest up on this comfortable lounge chair."

DJ lied down to rest and I put a movie on. Suesan and I snuggled as we both drifted off to sleep.

Chapter Eight:

Into Her Life

Suesan

While I was walking it was as if the night sky was creeping overhead. I was joined by the feelings of doubt, and shame... at least I think I was. Things were a little blurry. I heard a noise but didn't see from where it came. I didn't pay attention to it but it continued and I turn around to see a man standing only feet away from me. "Do you know who I am?" He asks. I'm sure I said no.

"Come with me and you won't ever be alone again. Do you want that?" I shake my head. "Then come with me." I start to follow but don't ask why. Why didn't I ask why? We pass several houses until there was none. At this point, my legs feel like baby deer legs and the guilt and shame continue to follow this strange man and myself. We come upon a faraway house with boarded windows, several panels lying on the ground, steps that are uneven and unstable. The house is too dark, not even a glistening sun could shine into the open spaces.

I follow him into this house, he didn't lock the door, he just walks in. We went up a narrow staircase to another door that he opens. He looked at me, insinuating that I walk in first. My legs feel like baby deer legs and suddenly, I lose total control of my feet but it wasn't my intoxication, no. There is a strange grab at the back of my neck. I can't move or run. As a matter of fact, at this point this dimly lit room was gyrating around me, my legs and arms are flailing and I'm rag dolled onto a bed. I wish I didn't take that last swig of liquid courage at this party. Even though it was my first time, they were saying I was doing such a good job. I wish I wasn't dizzy so I can see this man who for a little while didn't make me feel so alone. I wish I could remember the faces at the party. Coming back to myself, I can see this room has no windows, just four walls and a bed with an antique floor lamp towards one corner, my only source of light. By this time I was wavering, but standing. He closed the door and circled me like how I imagined an 18th-century slavery bid would be. He sat on the bed, "If I knew he would have you this drunk, I would have told him to stop." He laughs. "He said you know how to strip. Strip for me." He demands. I say no.

"Strip for me, now!"

I don't respond. My head keeps spinning. He stood up and locked the door and put the key under the bed. He was making a statement. "Strip for me or you're not getting out." I strip and still, I didn't ask myself why I was doing this.

Reluctantly I take one piece of clothing off at a time. First my shirt over my head, then my bra, sneakers, and pants. I could barely stand up let alone take my panties and my socks off. He looks at me and smiled, "You something else." Then he reaches under the bed. I looked around, this place started to look more familiar.

He takes two shot glasses out and pours liquor into them. My captor looks at me. "I reckon you already had enough." He drinks them both.

He tells me to go to him with the control of his fingers. I came to him and I did not ask why. He caresses my face and kisses me. His breath is hot and I still feel like I'm drinking. Why am I letting this happen? I tell him to stop then he keeps going and starts touching. This is where things get worse, this is where things are lost, and this is where those shadows of guilt and shame stop being entities that exist outside of me.

What I remember well is heat and light. A fire in the pit of my stomach and throughout the rest of my body. Not warm like a blanket, but hot like a stove. Not burning like a cup of hot cocoa but scalding like popping grease. He was so strong and heavy. What I remember some, was that lamp. Its shade a yearning red, textured and quiet with a pole that looked brass and royal. What was something like that doing in a place like this? Silent, with a dull light, as if it was a beacon slowly dying out.

The next thing I remember is being in that same top of the steps picking up my clothes that are thrown and scattered at my feet and the first few steps. I picked the pieces up and put them on. Oddly enough I wasn't as disgusted with the dirt on my feet from these neglected steps or the dust that was embossed on my bra and jeans now. I wasn't bothered by much of anything, but I couldn't even say bothered because it wasn't even that. I feel absent. A sense of being alone. It didn't go away.

I'm just thirteen. Only thirteen. My life as I had it is no longer coming back. I return home and never did see him again. I vow to not tell a soul. This secret will stay protected with me.

∼

My mother's name is Clarissa or "Clare Bear" according to my dad. She's about 5 foot 3 and her mother was Indian and her father was white. Although my mom is short, she has an assertive presence, and for that reason, my dad gravitated towards her. My mom has long curly hair which I try to imitate when I go out with my friends. She loves being around children so much she decided to become a teacher. My dad, on the other hand, is mixed. He works in the marketing department at a very big corporation. He's still pretty handsome too, even though his hair is now salt and peppered. My mom tells me stories of his charm, how he was funny, and adorable when they first met and I see he hasn't stopped being who she fell in love with since then.

My dad is learning how to run the corporation from grandpa who was running his company in Wilmington for over 30 years. His dad had to retire because he was getting too old and that was okay for my dad since he was accompanying grandpa to work since he was 12-years-old. But times have changed since he was 12 and my mom and I jokingly bother my dad by saying the only thing that has changed since he was a boy was his shoe size because he still thinks bellbottoms, and afros are hip, though his hair and pants are a slightly bit slimmer now.

When I get older I would like to major in psychology or do something that has to do with marketing like my dad. My life as I know it so far has been pretty good. I had trouble in elementary and middle school, but I'm adapting to the different changes in my life in high school and I'd like to think I grew up. My age doesn't reflect my history. Now that my family is paying more attention to me, I can slowly return to my rightful age and experiences. We are not rich but we sure are on our way. We are definitely rich with love that I longed for a very long time. After my dad finishes this big project, he said he's due to take over the company. I hope for the best with him and his project. My family is definitely a great one.

~

"Hey mom I'm home!" I greeted my mom in the dining room.

"Suesan baby, what's going on?" Mom asked as she kissed me on the cheek.

"Nothing really, I had fun at my friend's house." I replied as I get an apple from the counter.

"You didn't call to tell me that you were staying at her house, I had to call Pat's mother to know if you were staying the night. I called you but you didn't answer your phone. Whatever happened to calling me?" She asked stopping what she doing to look at me.

"Mom I'm sorry, I was not planning on staying, but one thing led to another then I fell asleep. I told Pat that I couldn't stay but it happened." I told her as I shrugged.

"It's alright, just don't do it again." Mother declares looking at me.

I went into the baby's room to see how my Gloria was doing. At 2 years old with long brown hair coming down her back she only cried when she didn't get her way. Gloria is a very smart and observant toddler. After I check on Gloria I go to check on my brother, Luis. He's in his room and he's the middle of all three. He looks just like me. I play with him in his room when I have to babysit and I love his personality. He's not like the other boys that are generally destructive and hardheaded. On the contrary, he's very calm and sweet. He plays with his toys like legos, blocks, and trucks. He's very smart for his age according to mom and his teacher and I think it's from everyone teaching him different things.

Next, I walk in to say hi to the oldest, Mark, who is much different than Luis. He likes guns, the woods, and army clothes. He also likes to read Hardy Boys books and so far he says that he wants to be a police officer or detective when he's older. Despite being rough, he likes to help out with Gloria.

Finally, I greet my sister Mia with a hug. As per usual, she's playing with her babies, putting them in different bonnets with matching onesies. She likes fashion, too. And a few times a week I can find her wrapped in different kinds of sheets and using our living room as her personal runway. I love them all. My brothers and sisters are special in their own way.

After coming home and playing and greeting everyone, I just took some time to be by myself. I went upstairs to my room. My room is purple and pink, with a king-sized bed and a large window that opens up into a balcony that opens out to the beach. I lie on my bed to think about Jahem. I feel so bad that I can't do anything to help him. I haven't seen him since I found out about Jaramia and I miss him a lot.

He's much better than Colton. Colton is so mean to people and only cares for his team and his Tuff Boys and not much else, not even me, the one he was supposed to protect. And look how he treated Jahem. Jahem is different. I keep bouncing these ideas back and forth until I fall asleep.

I wake up to my mom calling me to come downstairs to watch my sister. My house is bigger than Jahem's. It has two living rooms, a big kitchen, and a huge dining room. But my favorite part is the backyard and fountains.

When I walk into the kitchen Gloria is holding her hands out to me. "Come here Gloria, are you hungry?" She just laughed and put her hands out so I can pick her up.

"She shouldn't be hungry I just fed her while you were asleep." My mom concluded as she cut up the last of the apples for the boys.

"Well ok, I'll just give her a little bit so she can settle down. Maybe she'll take a nap." I walked into the kitchen to get the bottle.

"Okay, but like I said, don't feed her a lot." I put the bottle in the hot boiling pot as she continued to do 40 things at once. "Here boys, come and get your snacks. Suesan, you're going to have to stay here with your brothers and sisters all day today because I have a lot of errands to run." She said this while she put on her jacket. "Your father will be here later he told me, but you know him, straight upstairs to his study to work on this project."

"Mommy you know Suesan, she's going to be on the phone with her BOYFRIEND Jahem." Mia laughed.

"You know what, just for that, that's exactly what I'm going to do." We both stick out tongues out to each other in a teasing way.

"Look you two, I got to go. Be good and don't give your older sister a hard time."

"Okay mom." Mia said.

"As a matter of fact, Mia, go upstairs so I can take you to your friend's house. You weren't going to stay here anyway. I almost forgot."

"Oh thank you, thank you, thank you mommy." Mia gave mom a big hug and darted upstairs.

"That girl is crazy sometimes." Mom laughed.

"She's definitely your daughter." I said, as we both laughed and Mia came quickly down the stairs with her coat and a bag of toys and coloring books.

"Oh wow, would you look at the time, I have to go!" My mom rushed out with Mia behind her. We exchanged I love you's and I shut the door.

Watching my brothers and my sisters had been easy but this time was slightly different. This was my first time watching them alone. The only time that I watched them was when they were sleeping or when my mom was here or just stepped out for a few minutes. Now I have the opportunity to watch them all by myself. We watched cartoons for a long time. If it wasn't for me saying let's do something else, they'd watch Nickelodeon and the Disney Channel all afternoon.

Next they wanted to play Twister and they were pretty good for being so little. Good thing they know their colors and shapes. But Gloria just sat on the side of the mat touching their feet. I love her so much.

They eventually move onto another game and I stayed on the couch playing peek-a-boo with Gloria. They began to settle down one by one, either lying down on the couch, or Luis, the oldest, going into another room to play with his action figures. I warmed up more milk up for Gloria hoping that she'd finally take a nap too. I took Gloria and went to her room. I sat on the rocking chair and rocked her back and forth as I fed her. It took all of five minutes to get to her fully to sleep.

With all of the children occupied or sleeping, now I was able to do what I wanted for the next couple of hours.

RING.... RinG.... rINg. I picked up the phone, it was mom.

"Hello, Suesan," She said with that same frenzied energy from earlier, "Did your dad get home?"

"No, but I'm doing swell over here, no problems." I reassured her.

"Okay. Well if everything is good over there then tell your dad when he gets there that to call me if I'm not there before he comes. I will be home in an hour or two. It feels good to be Clarissa for a while and not mommy or Clare Bear. Thank you for taking care of the house for a while."

"Take your time. Everything is taken care of over here. Everyone ate and slept. But I will let him know when I see him." I replied.

"Thank you, my love." Mom said as she breathes deeply. "I know I can count on you."

I hung up with my mom and went into the living room with the leftover plate of ravioli and hotdogs I made for dinner. Luis and Mark were playing with the baby. Luis was holding Gloria between his legs and Mark was facing Gloria playing red hands. Mark and Luis were laughing really hard because Gloria kept missing it which made Gloria laugh.

RINg.... RiNg.... riNG....

"Hello."

"Hello sweetheart, this is Jahem." He said happily. He called to tell me about the results from court. "Court went well. They had found my father and he is up for sentencing now. He was at his sister's house. He blames it on the drinking and is pleading his innocence. He said that he didn't mean to hit her but what else is new."

"Did they ask what led to the fighting?" I pondered.

"Actually it's funny that you ask that question because honestly, I don't know. When it first happened, I thought it was because I saw you. However, I had to leave the courtroom and they never spoke of it again so I really don't know." He explained.

"How's your mother taking all of this?"

"What I respect about her is how resilient she is. She says that as long as she gets some type of money from this whole episode that she will be happy. She has a hospital bill along with all of the other house expenses to pay."

"How is your mom with Jaramia? Did she tell your father about him?"

"She didn't tell him about Jaramia. But they are both getting along quite well, Jaramia is actually speaking to her and just speaking more in general. You should come by the house and see them." I thought about the offer, it's been a long time since I've seen him and would love to be around him. I was so happy to finally be able to go back. Jahem made me feel so safe. I reassured him with a lot of enthusiasm because I think… I know he is the one for me. Colton who?

We talked for a while, and it was so nice to hear his voice. He was very excited to talk about him making the tryouts for football and basketball.

"Babe, I look forward to seeing you soon. I have to go. Kisses."

"Talk to you later. Mauh, mauh, mauh."

I sat down on the couch to think about Jahem and the way he made me feel. I should be used to this feeling but it still feels new.

"HEY I AM HOME, WHO WANTS A BEAR HUG OR WHO WANTS TO GET HUGGED BY THE BEAR???" My father said with his deep voice walking in the door with his arms stretching over his head and mouth wide open.

There he was in the doorway, standing 6 feet, light skinned with two bags in each hand. One bag contained a surprise for Mark and Luis. They were so happy to see him. Jumping around and carrying on as if it was their first time seeing him in forever. He's always the life of the party. I picked up Gloria who was happy to see him too and covered her eyes in excitement. I was happy to see him too.

"How is my babe, Gloria? I missed you so much, yes I did. I got a surprise for you."

He pulled out a unique looking rattle out of his right back pocket. This was one fancy rattle, with a twister and wheel in neon purple and pink.

"Do you have something for me, dad?" I asked wishing he did.

"Sure I do honey." He reaches into his bag and pulled out a dress. The dress had straps on the shoulders and straps crossed in the back. Purple and blue were my favorite colors and he knew just what to get. "I also have one more thing." He reaches in the bag and pulled out matching Chuck Taylors.

"What is all this for?" I wondered.

"This is for a very special day that is coming up and I want you to look nice." He smiled.

"Okay. Where am I going?" I said narrowing my eyes to his.

"It is a surprise. So don't wear it until I tell you" He stressed as he gave me the dress and shoebox to put in my room.

"Thank you," I responded as I turned to walk upstairs. "Oh dad," I turned back around, "momma said to call her. She called about an hour ago."

"Okay I will. But first, how about we all go get some pizza? I'm starving."

∼

We returned home to see my mother in the living room on the phone, I guess talking to a very important person. "My students need the best care in the classroom. That includes new books and technology." She saw us and waved warmly, but even the youngest of us knew that she was busy. "Hold on someone is on the other line…" My mother put her hand on her head stressed, "I will call you back." She clicks over as she shook her head looking at me, but smiling. "Hello… Who…Oh, Colton." My eyes became wide by the name I didn't to hear. Hers did too. "Yes, it's been a while… Suesan is right here. Hold on." I gave my mother a look that said why. She put the phone in my hand and took Gloria and the boys upstairs, telling me she'll finish her calls upstairs. "Call me if you need me." It was time for me to face the music.

"Hello." I said, trying to force out a normal greeting.

"Hey. Suesan. What is up with you lately? I haven't seen you around here. You know how I am about you. Are you okay?" Not to my surprise, he sounded drunk, even in prison.

"That's because you are in jail, or don't you remember?"

"OH. Ha." He paused to cough. "Yes I remember, so what are you doing?"

"I am just watching my siblings."

"Oh okay so when I get out, we going to see each other, right?"

"That depends if I am busy or not. School is getting tough"

"What you so busy with?"

"I'm busy with schoolwork and my family and stuff."

"I know what you mean. Right now I am trying to find out who put me in here. I paid this cop to give me some more dirt on my case. Some punk boy said that they saw me and my crew start the bar fight. But babe, I promise you, we didn't." He breathes slow and deep. "We didn't start no trouble. Everyone was drinking a little too much, and things just went too far. The man disrespected me, and you know I had to fix that." He said tiredly.

"Just be careful in there. Try not to get in any more trouble. But like I said, I have to go. You take care in there."

"Babe?" He said confused. I put the phone to my heart and closed my eyes. I heard the words slip his lips again and I hung up.

I go upstairs to take a shower. I needed some kind of washing for the guilt I felt after that conversation. I grabbed my robe and went onto my balcony to think. "When is too much too much?" I asked myself while I closed my eyes and feel the wind move through my body. I inhaled and exhaled and for a moment, I was happy. I just stood there, inhaling and exhaling until my pain finally turned into water streaming down my cheeks. I just stood there letting my burden wash upon my face. I opened my eyes and looked up to the sky and said a prayer. "If you are listening, please know I am still here…I am still here…Don't leave me right now. I need you. I am still here. In Jesus' name. Amen."

*Nothing fixes a thing so intensely in the memory
as the wish to forget it.*
-Michel de Montaigne

Chapter Nine:

Happy Birthday

Suesan

"Happy birthday to you, happy birthday to you, happy birthday dear Suesan, happy birthday to you. Blow out your candles honey, and make a wish."

I blow out my candles to a mini cake my dad had just brought into my room.

"And this is only the beginning, today and all your days are only going to get better." My dad says, as he put his hands on my shoulders. I wonder what he's up to. "But you will have to wait and find out. Right now your mother and I just made you breakfast." On cue, my brothers bring in my breakfast on two trays, eggs, pancakes, sausage, orange juice, and chocolate milk. "When you are completely finished, come downstairs. Don't peek or try to come down. I'm watching you." My dad says toying with me.

"Thank you boys. I appreciate your help." I give them both a hug as I look at the delicious food. After I ate, I went to brush my teeth and wash my face, hearing a happy commotion downstairs.

I head downstairs with the biggest smile on my face and to my surprise my dad was right. I saw a brown, black and white puppy with long ears and pretty big eyes. The pup had a pink bow around her neck and her coat was so long and fluffy. Talk about a birthday gift. I really enjoy and love puppies. She came to me and on the spot, I had called her Dayla. Dayla kept licking and jumping on the boys and they had fun with her. Gloria was reaching for the puppy while she was in my mother's hands.

I grab Gloria and bring her closer to see the dog who immediately starts to jump up at her and lick her hands.

"Are you happy with the pup?" Mom asks.

"Yes," I reply looking up at her, "SO happy, thank you SO much." I say this looking down at Gloria, Dayla, and my dad. I hug them all.

"Welp, your surprises are not over." Dad says gesturing outside.

"What you mean?" I ask as I hand Gloria to dad and slowly walk outside to see a black limo.

"Look, you can get dressed right now and have the whole day to yourself or you can spend time with your boring family and have the whole night to yourself. Your choice." Dad explains. I walk over to him and touch his shoulder.

"Dad, this family is not boring. However, I would want this day and limo all to myself." Dad and mom laugh.

"I thought so." My mother says. "Remember the dress your dad bought you? Go put that dress on then come back downstairs. And your last surprise will be inside the limo. Have fun and be safe love."

∽

When I enter the limo I see that I have a gift certificate for The Groove Room. "The Groove Room. This gift certificate allows the holder for unlimited food and fun all day."

I arrive at The Groove Room after telling my limo driver and I see a familiar face. This is very much a surprise. I walk over and greet Colton who is sitting at a booth alone. The smile on my face was screwed on tight and I felt like I couldn't breathe.

"How you doing, baby?" Colton asks as he wraps me in for a hard and strong hug.

"I am doing fine…" I respond as he hugs me and I attempt to show some kind of interest. This is not a birthday gift anymore. I know my parents meant well with allowing me to be here all day but now I'm doomed. "How did you get out of jail so early and so fast?"

"One of the head CO's at the jailhouse, Joe, the same one who let me know who ratted me out, said if I don't get in trouble for two more weeks that I can come outside for one whole day to see you." He says gloating as he fixes the ugly suit and tie. It wasn't that the suit was ugly but it didn't fit him right. The sleeves were the right length but he was swimming in it. Despite the fact he kept himself in shape, no one could help the crimped shoulder pads. He probably picked it up in a rush from the juvie rentals. "And well, here I am. So what you been up to? How's your family and friends, Brenda and Pat?" He asks but I don't want to reconnect. I should have stayed home but a smile is firmly on my face.

"Everything's good. It's like I told you on the phone, I just have been in my studies and taking care of Gloria and my siblings. And my friends are still crazy and funny as ever." I laugh. Hopefully, it doesn't sound too forced.

"Cool, let's eat. You look gorgeous by the way and you smell amazing." He waves down a waiter before I can say I'm not hungry.

"Colton, I am not really hungry. I ate before I came over here. I didn't know I was coming to The Groove Room." Colton looks at me and all I could think about is Jahem. It's nice to see Colton but I don't feel the same way about him. I wonder if I really feel anything at all.

"Okay. Well, I will just order, I'm hungry. It's hard to get Groove Room quality on the inside. We can still enjoy each other's presence."

"I'm sorry. I didn't know I was coming here until I got into the limo."

"No, it's okay. Your parents were reluctant to help me make your birthday special. I didn't understand why. I am your boyfriend after all. I assumed they had plans for you as well and didn't want to spoil it." He explains this as the waiter comes over to take his order. The rest of the time with him was slow with lots of dead air. I didn't want to be here and his time away didn't make me feel any different than I did before he went to jail. I thought I had a handle on not living in fear but I was wrong. I miss Jahem.

Being with Jahem opened my eyes to what being desired, cherished, and empowered felt like. Colton kept on speaking about some of our memories before he got locked up, every time starting with, "remember that time." I assume all he had to do in there was sit and think. My life had kept moving since he went to prison, and I'm starting to realize that Colton's energy just makes me think about negative things like death, and being someone's accessory. And then it came to me like a lost message: I realized that every day I was with him I had been losing a bit of me until he became the only reason I existed. I was protected but I wasn't myself. I was sure then and there that I needed more than that, I wanted to be my own person again and this wasn't the way to do it.

∼

After he finishes eating he looks up towards the entrance of the restaurant. I follow his gaze to a man in black. He looked very serious and I assume this is the person to take him back to jail. Colton walks me to my limo and kisses me on the cheek. "It was nice to see you, Suesan." I reply with a nod and sit in the limo. I could barely look Colton in the face. He keeps the door open for a little while before closing it. I feel him staring at me, but I didn't look towards him. Still looking straight I asked the driver to proceed to my next destination.

∼

My next destination was the school. There is a note and a red rose taped to the entrance door. I knew it was for me so I remove it and walk inside as I begin to read it.

I fell in love with you the first day I saw you in class. You didn't notice me, but I know noticed you. Although we were friends then, I'm so happy I have you now. Every date we went on was a blessing for me. Now, this day is about you. Happy Birthday.

"This is so cheesy." I say as I finish re-reading the letter. This is a nice gesture and I'm very flattered. I put it in my purse and admire the flower.

"I know this is cheesy." That voice. I look up but couldn't turn around. I was frozen. "But this is the first place where I fell head over heels for you. Happy birthday."

I turn around to see the person that I've been wanting and waiting to see. He wore a navy blue suit with a white shirt open at the collar, and the same glasses from the day he first drove his car to school. Classic, sexy, a bit cheesy, but romantic.

"Jahem." I breathe out his name and just stare at him. "How are you?" I ask as I gradually start to walk to him which eventually led to me running.

"I am doing so much better now." As he lifts me up and spins me around.

"I am so glad to see you." I say amazed. I felt as though I looked at him like I had not seen him in years. He means a lot to me. I kiss him and it feels like I'm in a book.

"I am glad that you approve." He grabs my hand and helps me get into the limo. "So how was your day so far?" He asks.

"It was fine until I saw Colton." I didn't look at him when I said his name. Looking out the window, I continue before he could say anything. "We didn't do anything. And I didn't expect to see him. It was a surprise and my family was forced into it by Colton. They didn't want to reveal anything that I wasn't ready to face. But the person that I wanted to see was you. I did not feel right being there with him. I'm sure he felt that." I reach for his face. "He doesn't know about us. It was just for today. He's back in jail now."

"Yes, but I thought they don't do that kind of stuff. They let him out for a whole day?" He looked worried.

"Well, he told me that the head correction offer said if he stayed out of trouble that he will let him out."

"Wow, well I hope he won't get out again." He says this clasping his hands to his face.

"He should not have a reason to." And Jahem nods his head. I change the conversation. "Where are you taking me?"

"You have to wait and see." He pulls me in to give me a smooch and tells the limo driver to drive.

We spent most of our time laughing and walking on the beach. I can't ever get enough of walking through Wrightsville Beach with him. It started to become late, so we returned to the limo and decided to go to another restaurant. We were very hungry as we rode up to Midnight Locks, which was a couple of minutes away from the beach and my house. If you come here at night and wait here until 12 midnight something special happens. The owner built the restaurant just behind the weeping willow tree that stands tall in front of the establishment, towering over outside tables and chairs. I heard about this place. He believes the tree is enchanted and that if you lock your dreams in it, your dream will come true. Something about the moon carrying a stronger wind from the ocean that carries the "essential lunar energy from the heavens," according to the plaque by the tree.

"I love this place. This is my second favorite restaurant. Does it fit you Suesan?" Jahem asked, staring passionately into my eyes, but through my soul.

"Yes." I said softly. "But this looks very expensive."

"Don't worry about it. I got some money from my mom. She says happy birthday." He said as he opened the door to the restaurant. "She wanted to make your day as special as you are. She is thanking you for helping her when she needed it the most. She wants to make this the best day of your life."

"I am thankful for you and your mother." We followed the waiter to our seats, but before we sat down Jahem had something else in mind.

"Come with me." He motioned as he glided his hands down the middle of my back and my hairs stood up. "I want to show you why this place is so wonderful." We walked into a room with no door. It was full of trees in pots hanging over each other in the room.

Jahem walked me over to one of the planted trees. "This is a weeping willow." He gestured as he touched one of the branches. "This tree is known for being the tree of dreaming, intuition, and deep emotions. If you lock two branches together..." He explained as he demonstrated, "and close your eyes and whisper what your dream or wish is," Jahem was quiet for a moment and slowly spoke to the willow, "then your dream will magically transform into your reality."

He opened his eyes and looked at me. "Suesan..." He looked at the tree. "This weeping willow tree is also for healing." He took my hands. "The willow opens up a door to help a person move through different painful emotions like sadness, grief, loss, and external hardship related to inner pain, like tears and depression. The willow aids the healing process."

"Thank you." These are the only words that I can utter.

"I know you have been through a lot. I don't know the ins and outs of your life but I do know you are a strong person. All I want to do is help you." He looked back at the tree. "Try it...for yourself."

I took the two branches and braided them together. I thought, "I want peace. I want this darkness to leave me. I dream of being back to myself. I want to be whole, again...please?" I quietly asked the weeping willow tree. If Jahem believes, so will I. I started to tear. Jahem slowly gave me a hug.

"Let's get back to the brighter part of your birthday now, shall we?" He grabbed my hands and led me to our table. As he sat across from me, he wiped the last remaining tears from my broken eyes, and as he did I realized...I loved him. I love him. But I couldn't tell him. I hope this weeping willow really is enchanted. I quickly grabbed the menu as he reached for his. I put the menu close to my face. What the fuck. I love him. Does he even love me? Am I worthy of this emotion I feel? My life is not ready for my added pressure. I shouldn't love anyone, not even Jahem. He has been so nice to me but there is so much he doesn't know about me. What would he think if I told him who I really am inside? When did this get complicated? My inner thoughts wouldn't let me enjoy what I had in front of me at this moment. I soon collected myself. I had no other choice. Jahem is right here, let me enjoy him.

"This place is beautiful." Saying the first thing that came to my head.

"Yeah is it." Jahem concurred while looking around. He looked back at the menu. "Is there anything that sounds interesting to you?" He looked up for my answer.

"Yes, the chicken and potatoes. I am starving."

"Well, I'm actually glad you didn't eat anything with Colton. Now you can pig out all you want here." He chuckled.

"Excuse me, do you want to order?" The server asked.

"Yes, I want your chicken special for the lady and for me the roasted chicken and vegetables."

"Right away." She said as she took our menus.

"So Suesan, how did you like the letter I wrote to you?"

"I love the letter a lot, and the rose. Thank you."

"That's good because I got something else for you." He signaled for someone to come over. "Now close your eyes and hold out your hands." As I held out my hand I felt something drop in my hand. A small box covered in soft material with edges that felt like stones. "Okay, open your eyes."

As I opened my eyes, the box was gray with small stones around it. I opened the box to see a necklace filled with blue diamonds in the center and a gold pendant around them. As I looked down I saw there were dozens of lilies on the table. He remembered my favorite flower, too.

I looked up from the flowers with so much happiness. "Thank you Jahem." I said thoughtfully. "This really has been a great day for me. I really do feel special." I reached across the table to give him a kiss.

"Here you both go." The waiter said putting our plates in front of us.

"You're welcome Suesan. I just want you to have the best day ever. So if you're with me, you have nothing to worry about."

"I love how you make me feel secure." He looked at me in great thought. I wonder what he's thinking.

After the food came we ate our food in silence, but it was a good silence... I think. Something began to shift. Or was it me? Once we were done he picked up the check and we left and he grabbed my hands and we exited the restaurant.

"Are we okay?" I asked as I followed him out of the restaurant holding his hands. He didn't respond. I stopped him from walking and looked in his eyes.

"Look, Suesan I am not mad or anything. I am alright." Jahem said reassuringly. "I was never mad okay. I was just being quiet." Jahem opened the door to the car. "Well, we just ate and I'm not ready for this night to end. You have on a stunning dress on and I have on a nice suit, so..." He said smiling with his eyes.

∽

Jahem surprised me by taking me to a jazz club. We both admired instrumental jazz. He loved the saxophone and I loved the guitar. I had never been to The Life of Music with friends because I haven't had anyone to share the experience with besides my parents. Colton doesn't appreciate such art but I am blessed to share this with Jahem. I love jazz with my soul. Who wouldn't fall in love with the rhythmic, poetic, and soul grabbing journey of a smooth sax and a swinging snare drum? The Life of Music has a stage filled with professional musicians. On different days I've come here with my dad to listen to artists share their poems, music, or art.

"Is this everything you imagined?" Jahem asked holding me from behind. I just nodded in utter bliss. "Let's go grab a table and I will get us something to drink." Jahem pointed to a nice corner set up. We quickly walked over to the table. "Coke, right?"

The place was nice and calming. Everyone was talking and laughing but never got noisy. Couples were cuddled up and even those who looked single were having a good time. I've never been to another place that matched the soothing to the eyes and soul feeling of this club.

"Here you go Suesan, and guess what?" He asked, sitting down beside me whispering in my ear

"What." I whispered back.

"I know the bartender and he said that he will give us two drinks for free." He said proudly.

The announcer came on, "Hello everyone. Welcome to another night at Life of Music. I am your host, Maxell. We have an awesome line up for everyone today. So let's jump right into it. Enjoy."

Everyone that went up was so wonderful. The artwork was beautiful and the poems were transparent, sad, exciting, dangerous, and moving. I was so taken aback and I never felt so connected with other people's emotions and pain. As the night went on, I rode through this journey that took me so many places in my soul I didn't even know existed.

"The next performer is from our hometown, please welcome this new artist to The Life of Music, Suesan." Maxell started clapping and I suddenly became frozen. I quickly realized he was talking about me. I looked at Jahem and was wondering what was going on.

"Go on ahead." He said supportively. "I know you write and I want to hear you."

"Come on everyone. She is shy. Welcome her to the stage." Maxell stated. He started to clap again along with the rest of the room.

"I am here. Just look at me. No one else." Jahem touched my hands and pulled me on my feet.

"I love you, Jahem."

"I love you too, Suesan." We had a long embrace and then I walked up to the stage, no longer nervous.

"Hi everyone...Today's my birthday and this was a surprise set up by my boyfriend Jahem." Everyone started whooping and hollering when I said it was my birthday. When the claps settled, I continued. "I write poems and I would like to share it with everyone. I don't have a title yet but please bear with me." I stared at Jahem as I exhaled and the words came rushing out:

Yahne Sneed

*The words flow
and I kept my eyes fixed on him.*

*Never letting go
of the warmth I felt within them.*

*I speak life into my microphone
hoping my heart will leave me alone.*

*But yet I pour my heart out and cry
When all I wanted to do was fly.*

*Fly away from these emotions I felt,
To stay in his arms and disappear into his chest.*

*To feel his heart and forget about mine.
I miss being up on stage, where everything is fine*

*I miss leaving my heart up here
beating with emotions that I can't control.*

*But this something was different, something in the air
I felt my heart heal, and my past, I no longer cared.*

*So now I can wrap myself in bandages,
recover from my pain that will soon be over.*

*He is more than what I need.
He is what helps me breathe.*

*And now there's no more to explain…
because now I'm freed from my own chains*

Chapter Ten:

Pandora's Box

Jahem

Time has flown by and so much has happened since Jaramia came to stay with us. I'm 18 now and my family including Suesan and DJ all had special party plans for us to do. My mom and brother took me to the movies and Red Lobster, then I went parasailing and skydiving with DJ. Suesan and I went on a weekend cruise too, courtesy of both of our families. Out of everything, I enjoyed spending these two years with Suesan without much worry. Our bond is so strong.

But little did I know, my life would soon be changing again very suddenly. We kept each other distracted with school and living life, but the beat of my heart grew faster and faster as the inevitable was bound to happen. Colton kept in touch with Sue to inform her of any changes to his case. When Suesan told me he was mentioning coming home to her soon, I didn't think much of it. But, word on the street was that Colton and some of his boys were being released soon on good behavior. I didn't think it was possible. His crew, yeah, maybe they'd be out. But not Colton.

"Yo, I can't believe it, he had two whole years left. I didn't expect this." DJ says, shocked as he taps my leg and holds up a two with his other hand. I notice it's the same sign as a peace sign. I wish there'd be peace. "What you think he's going to do? Anything and everything can happen with him out. Groups would probably be reformed." Doren adds, as he got up to get more chips. Since Colton went to prison, the high school was a whole lot safer, too. No more small gangs or much bullying. And now that DJ, Suesan, and I were seniors, our class set the tone for the rest of the school.

"Look it'll be alright," I say calmly, "What we need to do is stay out of his way..." I say turning to DJ. "Also, don't tell him about Suesan and me."

"You know I won't say anything. You can trust that." DJ concurs, as he eats his refilled bowl of chips. "But you know what...the school knows and if the school knows so do the Tuff Boys. Suesan needs to tell him before someone else does."

"I'm thirsty Jahem." Jaramia says, as he plops on the seat right next to me.

"Okay, one moment, Jaramia." I go into the kitchen to make him a turkey sandwich and chips to go with his juice. "Here you go." I give Jaramia a hug and off he goes.

"We should go to Suesan's house and see how she's holding up. I mean, you don't have to. But if she was my girl, I would."

"Yeah you're right, let me just tell my mom and grab my coat."

"Okay, I'll wait for you outside."

Mom was upstairs lying down in her room. I told my mom that I was leaving.

∽

"Come in boys, how are you doing?" Clarissa asked us.

"We are fine." We both said, as we sat down across from each other in the living room to wait for Suesan.

"Hey, Doren and Jahem." Suesan greeted us as she kissed me and gave DJ a hug.

"So...um-" Doren tried to speak, clearing his throat.

"Look you guys I know already. Yes, I am a little freaked out but I will live to see another day. Maybe he did leave with good behavior. How do you know?"

"Suesan, baby, we know because we know Colton. Colton is not some guy that went to jail because he was innocent. He went to jail because he is violent. Okay?" I say this, holding her hand looking into her eyes hoping she understands the situation.

"To make matters worse, he got out two years early. For good behavior? No, no, no. That's not right." Doren stressed. "You know he has an attitude problem and can't control himself. There's no way this makes any sense." Doren added.

"I know you guys." Suesan sighed as she sat back in the chair. "But what can we do?"

"Act calmly, act... natural." I said, as if I discovered something new. "Meaning, no relationship. He can't know."

"Agreed." Added Doren as we both looked at Suesan.

"Suesan, you agree right?" I asked.

"What happens if he notices something's wrong?"

"He won't, if we act natural, right?" I tried to be as reassuring as I possibly could. Deep down I knew it was only a matter of time before Colton found out. But there is no way I'm bothering Suesan's pretty face about him.

"Okay I trust you..." Suesan took a slow deep breath then nodded. "Agreed."

"Now that that is settled, where are your siblings?" I wondered looking around.

"On vacation. Not far as I'd hoped. Spending some time at my aunt's house. Right now they are at the beach. I am glad they are, more room for me to relax."

"Only if I could-" Doren got interrupted by a phone call. It was his mom. Doren left the living room and walked outside the house. He later came back inside and said he had to go ten minutes later. But I was not letting him go alone. I gave Susan a kiss and headed out the door when she stopped me and DJ and invited herself along for the ride. All of us continued to get closer and closer over the past 2 years. They're really like family and it was all so natural that it didn't bother us when she invited herself.

"Mom? Are you okay? Dad where are you?"

"Doren, I'm over here, help me. I am stuck." Doren's mom said this faintly and she sounded close but didn't sound well.

"What happened to you?" As he ran to his mom. "Where's dad?" DJ yelled and cried as his voice started to crack. Everything around me started to move faster.

"It happened again. They threw a rock into our window and it shattered the china glass. When I tried to take cover, I slipped on the broken china. Getting up, I leaned on the dresser and it fell on me." She said as she wiped her eyes. "Your dad is not here, he left to the store before this happened."

"Can you move your legs, Ma?"

"Yes, but it hurts a lot. I think it's swelling. I am going to help you push this off of me."

"No mom. Jahem and Suesan are here. They will help me." As Doren talked to his mom, it was very hard to see her like that. I walked over to DJ as he started to grab the dresser. Doren and I counted to 3, while Suesan grabbed his mother by the arms to pull her out from under the dresser. The first time, it did not work but we tried again and succeeded. Doren and I helped her to the couch. Her legs were very bruised.

"Are you okay, Ma?" Doren said, giving her a hug.

"Yes, I am okay. Just go call your father."

As he held on to his mother's hand and dialed with the other, I looked to Suesan because this was the first time we experienced this moment with her.

"Doren, I'm going to speak to Suesan over in the kitchen for a bit, I'll be back." I motioned Suesan into the kitchen with a head nod.

"I'm sorry this happened to you, Ms. Martha." Suesan said, wiping her eyes. It saddens me to see others feel anything but happy.

I brought Suesan in the other room away from Doren and his mother. Martha looked at Doren and Doren looked at Martha. No one said anything, their tears spoke a thousand words.

"When DJ first came to this school, Suesan, everyone didn't take well to him because of the color of his skin. They were mean, to say the least. The students didn't want him to go to their school but he did not want to leave. Especially when his mother paid a lot for them to get to where they were now. So to teach him a lesson, they threw rocks at his house with disregard to anyone in here." I paused to look at Suesan. "It's been a while, I thought they had given up after all this time. Everyone believes he doesn't belong. I am the only person that didn't turn him away because he's white." I looked at DJ. "His skin doesn't determine our friendship, his actions do." I looked back at Suesan. "Different isn't always wrong."

Suesan didn't respond but yet held my hands. I kept looking at Suesan and smiled warmly.

"He is blessed to have a family like you."

"No, baby. I'm blessed. We might be different shades of human but he is definitely my brother."

"But don't worry, I'm doing fine." DJ cut in as he walked into the kitchen to wash his hands. "They don't bother me. I'm going to be me in this skin as I would in darker skin. I will never please those who see me as less. "They are just aggravating." Doren said, as he walked toward us.

The door to the house opened up and entered Dave, Doren's father.

"Hey everyone." He said, looking in towards us, then at Martha. "Are you okay, hun?"

"I'm okay, I called Doren before anything else could happen. He came right on time."

He was very worried. He stood two inches taller than me and very red. He walked over to Martha and gave her a hug. Suesan, Doren and I left Martha with Dave and went back to my house. Doren needed to leave. I felt like coming with me was removing him from the situation. He almost had it rougher than me since moving here.

∼

"Now that I am thinking about it, do you think you should have left them by themselves?" Asked Suesan.

"No, it's best if they stay by themselves to bond and what not. They know I am safe." DJ said seriously, looking out of the window.

Everyone came in and laid on the couch. I was sleepy, lying on the couch, as DJ and I watched television. Suesan was laying on me drifting off to sleep. We woke up the next morning to a quiet house. My mom was off to work and Jaramia was in his room still asleep. We fixed us bowls of cereal. Everyone wanted to go home, so I dropped them off.

I later took Jaramia to the park and let him play with the other kids. I knew most of the parents and asked them to watch after Jaramia if he was on the other side of the park away from me. I must have dozed off because I woke up the exact time everyone was getting ready to leave. The park was being emptied by the mothers and fathers walking with their children to their cars.

"Come on Jaramia we are leaving." I said, walking over to grab his hand.

"I am sleepy big brother, pick me up. Can we get something to eat?" Jaramia asked tiredly. I just shook my head, smiled, and picked him up. When we returned home, I made a quick dinner: chicken nuggets and french fries in the oven, then tucked him in once he finished eating. He had fun, my mom is home, everyone is safe and now I can rest.

Chapter Eleven:

Set Me Free

Jahem

There are simultaneous cheers coming from inside the locker room and outside on the court. "OKAY LET'S GET READY. COME ON NOW LETS CHEER. CLO-VERS CLO-VERS CLO-VERS CLO-VERS."

"LADIES AND GENTLEMEN ARE YOU READY FOR THE CLOVERS? IF YOU'RE READY LET ME HEAR YOU SCREEEEEAAAAM!"

"Okay, look team. We can beat them. We've been going over the Lion's film for the past two weeks. We have the advantage as long as we stick to our plays and pass the ball. Be a team!! Let's Go!" The coach leads us out of the locker room and into the crowd. Walking onto the court, I'm focused but I scan the cheering fans. I see Suesan with her girls in their cheerleading outfits. I wave at her and she blows me a kiss. I then looked for our family in the stands and I wave at all of them. They're all holding a banner with my name across it. I put my jersey in my shorts and brush the nerves off. I was ready for the tip-off.

The referee holds the ball in position and throws it up in the air. My teammate smacks the ball my way. I cross one Lion, I cross another and I'm open at the top of the key. I pull up and sink the first two points for the Clovers. That was pretty clever but I'll be sure not to showboat and keep the ball moving. Still, not bad.

By the end of the first quarter, they were down by 5. The score was 32 to 27 when I look at the game clock and sweat is pouring down my face, we break for water and coach is writing on his pad. I sit down while the Clover cheerleaders cheer happy and proud. Suesan's eyes lock on mine, while they took their positions on the court. She counts off and they start cheering: "GO Jahem! GO Jahem! GO Clovers, GO Clovers!" Then they run to the whole team and shake their pompoms in our faces.

"Suesan." I say smirking, "Are you giving me support or distracting me?"

"Nope. I'm not distracting you. Just helping you focus." Suesan giggles and starts to backpedal away.

"I'm focused on something alright…But it's not this game I say a bit louder so she can hear me." She shakes her head laughing and skips away.

The buzzer goes off and now the second half starts. Feeling hydrated and refreshed I am ready to play again. The second half the Lions catch up. It was 56 to 55 with 20 seconds left to spare. A guy on my team makes a point. And on the transition, I intercept a pass and pick up speed. I run into a Lion's jersey but I recover and keep dribbling down the court but I hear a whistle as I take my layup. It goes in.

"Foul? On who?" I ask the ref. "I was all by myself!"

"Not you." The ref says. "Foul on the Lions. Two shots." If I make these two shots we will win. Referee passes me the ball. It bounces once, twice. I look towards Suesan who has her fingers crossed. Yes, the ball went in! 56 points to 56 points. Now we are all tied up. The ref passes me the ball again. "Okay this is it. People are counting on me. I need to make it." I tell myself. The whole gym is silent. I bounce the ball once and close my eyes and release the ball. It slowly hits off the backboard, bounces in and out around of the rim. But then goes in the net. Yes! We make it to the championships!

"GO CLOVERS. GO CLOVERS. GO CLOVERS. GO… GO… GO. GO CLOVERS. WOOOO WE'RE THE BEST!"

The feeling is so good. The school rushes to the court and I get hoisted up. Everyone is high fiving. The crowd is yelling and screaming. Happy team, happy coach. We finally win.

"I am so proud of you, Jahem". My mom said kissing me on my face while my brother was still cheering by her side and pretending he was dribbling a ball. She hugged me and said, "I see you later. Enjoy the victory."

"Thanks! Mom. Love you." I said as I gave her a hug after Jaramia.

"O man, I'm tired. Can we go for a walk?" I gestured to Suesan, and laughed in exhaustion as she ran to me to give me a squeeze.

As we walked out of the building there was a group of girls from her cheerleading squad that seemed to be following us out and they all seemed to be talking about my last shot. Suesan tried to tell them that she just wanted to be alone with me for a while but they weren't taking a hint, they were making it clear that they weren't leaving. This made her really mad. Suesan stood in front of me and broke any thought of connection the girls would have between their hands and my arms.

"Look, you all know he is with me and we were going for a walk—alone. Now it's time for everyone to leave and go home." Suesan gestured playing off the fact they didn't listen the first time. A girl that Suesan has never been friendly with pushed herself to the front of the group and looked at Suesan in the eyes.

"He is not even yours...unless his name is Colton." She looked at me. "And from where I am at, this is not Colton so he isn't yours. Isn't your real boyfriend getting out of jail soon?"

"The funny thing is..." Suesan moved closer to her face. "If I say he's mine, then he's mine and I'll appreciate it if you back the hell off. Do you really want to see what happens if you don't?" Suesan's ears started to get red.

"C'mon, Suesan, let's get up out of here." I grabbed her by her waist and pulled her away and we headed to the car. I had to break up a fight, especially between her and half the cheerleading team. Sue needed my protection.

We looked at each other in the car and I almost wanted to laugh but I just smirked. Though the situation was tense, Suesan would really throw down for me and that made me know that she was the one.

Her phone rang and it sounded very rushed. She hung up the phone and looked at me.

"My mother said that we are having our family reunion. I forgot. Do you want to come with me?"

"Sure. Your home it is. I'll go home and shower and be there in a little bit."

∼

I arrive at Suesan's house about an hour later and knock on the door. "Hey Clarissa. How are you today?"

She hugs me. At this point, I am very comfortable with Suesan's whole household. "Congratulations on your win Jahem, Suesan was telling me all about it. She's outside with her sister in the back." Clarissa points toward the backdoor.

I walk through the house and say hi to the guests scattered in different pockets of the rooms, some at the tables, couches, or chairs used as accent pieces in empty corners. I wave down Suesan, "Jahem. Come in, it just started." Suesan gestured.

"Everyone, this is my very close friend, Jahem Thomas. Jahem, this is my family. You already know a few of them but I'll introduce you to the others you don't know." Suesan places her hands on my shoulders as she brings me over to the different clusters of aunts, uncles, cousins, and elders. Under any other circumstance, this would've been great, but I couldn't help but feel all of their eyes on me in the most suspicious of ways. They must know about Colton.

"You want to dance?" I ask her as I take her by the hand onto the dance floor that was created by her dad. The floors were glossy red with four tall wooden pillars wrapped in beautiful bright lights that twinkled like stars. Everyone is laughing and carrying on in this peaceful reunion. I got closer to Suesan as the night breezed on by. I was just happy to be there with her. We laughed and talked about her family. And this was another perfect day until I felt a tap on my shoulder. I turned around and heard a familiar voice.

"Hey um… What are y'all doing? Don't get me wrong, I'm not mad." Colton says with an interesting amount of curiosity and calm.

"I'm…" I look at Suesan. "We were talking and enjoying the music. Friends can do that, so let's not cause any problems here. We both want Suesan time." I put my drink down and look at Colton. "But this is Sue's parents' house, let's try to remain civil. If you want to excuse yourself with her, then say it." I continue to stare down Colton. He doesn't scare me anymore.

"WAIT…" Squealed Suesan reaching for my hand without thinking.

"Suesan, I just want to talk or dance with you. I haven't seen you in a long time." Colton pleads looking away from me to her. "Do you think we can do that?"

"Sure." Suesan looks at me with an, *I don't want to leave you* look.

"Good looking out Jahem, props." Colton says while he pats me on the back. "Thanks for not letting her get into trouble."

"No problem?" I say this like a question but I didn't mean to. Helpless, I just watch the two of them start to walk off and he puts his arm around her as they turn passed a fountain and out of my field of vision. I lean up against the wall. Man, Suesan needs to tell him it's over and I hope she does soon. I walk over to some of the cousins to not appear so awkward.

∽

"Where did you come from Colton?"

"Suesan I know you know by now that I got out for good behavior." I did not say anything but he could see the look on my face. "You don't think I bribed someone to let me out, do you?"

"Did I say that? I didn't say that." I was trying to string this conversation on as civil as I could but I was glancing over now and again to see if Jahem was around.

"You sure not happy to see me, I see."

"Oh. I had a lot of things on my mind. That's all."

"Want to talk about it?" Colton says with a furrowed brow.

"No, not really." I say, still trying to spot Jahem.

"I just came back to spend time with you. I miss you. It's been rough."

"You just can't come back here and expect everything to be okay. A lot has changed, Colton."

"You are right, that is true. But I can try to prove to you that I've changed. Can I?" I think that was a question because in my own thinking I notice he was waiting for an answer. "So what up with Jahem?"

"What about him?" I question, looking at him.

"He seems to be everywhere that you are and on your mind. Don't try to deny it. I know you." He says this assertively. "When I left he was not your friend. Now here he is." He says in a whisper pointing down with his finger. "I heard what happened to his mother. Don't feel bad for that punk, his mother's face healed. She can take a hit."

"Do you hear yourself, Colton?! I continue to grow after you left and you remained the same. You need to lay off him." He hit a nerve. "Let me ask you something."

"Anything. I'm open with you." Colton says confident but taken aback. He never saw this side of me before. Not towards him, or anyone.

"What's your problem with him anyway? I have not witnessed him do anything wrong to you."

"I don't want to talk about it." Colton became very defensive and shut down completely which wasn't like the Colton I knew.

"Look we have been dancing and talking for a long time."

"And?" He questions with an attitude.

"Well the reunion is almost over, so I would like to mingle with the rest of my family." I stop dancing mid-song.

"So what about me?"

"This is all a bit too much. You're just getting out of jail and you just show up in the middle of my family reunion. And you are questioning me about you… You can stay or you can leave I don't really care."

"Okay, I will go. But it's only to just give you a piece of mind." He says, sounding hurt.

I look back at him and turn forward to look at Jahem. "Thank you."

∼

I see Suesan as she walks over to me a bit bothered, definitely confused.

"Are you okay, what happened?" As I hug her for reassurance I feel Colton staring at me but I didn't look in his direction.

"He didn't do anything. We just talked."

"Okay so what do you want to do now that that's over?"

"Let's go upstairs, Jahem, it's too much for me out here. I think I need a break. Don't follow me in. Wait about five minutes then come inside."

"Okay. Do you want anything to take with us upstairs?"

"Yes, a soda. I'll go say bye to everyone, okay?"

∼

"Thanks." Suesan says, grabbing the soda.

"You're welcome. Are you okay? Talk to me, baby."

"Yeah I'm fine it's just that a lot has happened while Colton was gone, and now he's back adding to all of the drama and everything... it's a lot." Suesan said laying her head on my shoulder.

"Yeah I know. But I want you to know I'm here to help."

"How can you, if Colton keeps showing up like he did today? We can't see each other."

"Sue, I will protect you and support you in any decision you make. But you have to understand that this will not go away unless you speak up." I grab Suesan's hands and pull her close. "I'm not defending Colton. However, Colton is only acting as a boyfriend would because that is who he believes he is until he knows differently. He can't act any other way babe…Sue, I said I'll protect you." I lift Suesan's head up to find her eyes. "I will be doing more damage than good to protect you.

My love for you has deepened. You have to tell him and soon. That's the only way." I hug her because I know she needs it. Hell, I need it too. "He doesn't know we are together. He may even think that I'm a nuisance."

"Yeah, you're right." Suesan looks at me. "You. Are. Right. I just need time." I give her a kiss. She kisses me back.

"I know we made love before plenty of times. But today with Colton, I don't know if I'm comfortable with this."

"Colton doesn't change how I feel for you Jahem. You are the only one to help me feel safe, confident, and not alone." Suesan kisses me again and lightly caresses my navel. She whispers, "I want this. I want you."

Like a song we began to undress each other routinely, the way the hook always comes before the chorus. Slow and steady we lie each other down. Suesan pulls my neck toward hers. She closes her eyes as we melt into each other and we share a connection that can't tear us apart.

Chapter Twelve:

Moving On

Suesan

"Look, I don't care if it's been a couple of weeks since the family reunion and I did not tell anyone, but you need to leave that child alone, they don't need this from you."

"I am your husband, Clarissa, for better or for worse, which also includes our child. I can't believe it. Why? Just why?"

"There is no need to push the cause, okay? Just let it die down in time and be there for the child, okay? He is a good boy and we raised a bright child. We will work this out."

Anthony's voice sounds wavering, "Clarissa that is unlike me. Unlike what our family is. I am very uncomfortable--Clarissa, this is our child. Our baby. How many times have we looked away?"

∼

I have to get out. It's my life. Why can't I be me? There is nothing they can do now. It's just as mom said, they need to just relax. I can't. I can't. I couldn't breathe, my body was rejecting everything I ate. I have to breathe. I can't keep meeting the toilet like this. Ugh, my head aches a lot.

I slowly drag my legs close to me to push myself off the toilet that I keep marrying with my face. Slowly I regain my strength and I get up off the floor. I wipe my mouth with a cold rag and gently dab it around my neck.

I'm leaving I am putting on my clothes. I really do not want to come back here. I stagger through my room to put on random clothes I find lying around.

I open my window, climb down the tree, and walk into the cold. It's crazy how I choose this day to clear my head, in this weather, it sucks.

I come around the corner tearing and tired. I see someone that I didn't expect to see.

"Hey you." I wave to DJ.

"Hey Suesan." DJ walks over to give me a hug.

"How is your mom?"

"She's fine, her leg healed and she is walking again." DJ says proudly as we walk together to nowhere.

"That's...That's great DJ." I say swallowing every ounce of vomit that's trying to come back to choke me.

"What's wrong with you?"

"Nothing it's just my dad found out and..." I start to tear again.

"How bad is it?" DJ ponders as he holds my hands walking me to the benches in the park.

"Well, he was yelling at my mom and tried to talk to me and I didn't give him a chance to. I didn't want to feel like I should be punished for something I did months ago. I have no right getting pregnant at this point in my life. I feel so ashamed of what transpired between Jahem and me. I mess up everything I touch. One decision that I made has already complicated my life in more ways than I can count. My dad is so disappointed in me. I didn't want to stay in that house. It was filled with so much sadness. I couldn't bear it so I climbed out my window."

"Ooo...Your hormones got you acting dangerous. I am scared of you." DJ and I laugh. "But honestly, how are you taking all of this?"

"I don't know what to do. In a way I am excited. I love Jahem. But I am afraid."

"Don't be. If your dad doesn't understand you, you have people that do. Does Jahem know the situation?"

"Well that's part of the reason why I am afraid. No, I did not tell him." I say slowly and sadly.

"That's okay, I will be right here when you are ready. Come here." Doren says as he gives me a hug. I give him a hug and then he kisses me.

We both move back and stare at each other. Through all the love that I have for Jahem, he did not come into my head when I kissed Doren back and I knew it was wrong. I think.

Between me feeling down and Doren being here when I needed someone to talk to, I just could not tell him to stop. DJ kissed me again. I needed to feel anything other than my own aching heart.

One thing leads to another and his hands slowly made their way under my shirt. The only thing that stopped things from heating up in the park was a loud man honking his horn at a car blocking his way to drive up the street. We both became startled and looked at each other. We both laughed.

"Look Suesan, I know how much you love Jahem and he is like a brother to me. I don't want to hurt his feelings, okay? Now that I am thinking with the right head, I know what we did was wrong. We have always been there for each other and we got caught up in the moment. You are beautiful but we are nothing more than friends. We both know that."

"Yeah, I know. So let's not talk or seem like we had anything to feel guilty about. It stops here and we won't do it ever again. We both love Jahem and that's the end of it, cool?" I say this as I hold my hand out and DJ returns the handshake.

"But I do have one question." He looks me in my eyes and I don't turn away. "Do you regret it?"

I take a deep breath and say, "No, no I didn't."

"Good. I didn't either."

"You were here in the moment, but. It. Ends. Here. I was not or am not abusing you as a friend. But thank you for being here. I belong to Jahem and that is where I will stay."

"I know you weren't abusing anything. I don't want anything else but your friendship and you are welcome."

After a couple of minutes, DJ walks me back to my house and I just stare at the house anticipating the walk of shame.

"Do you think they will yell at you?"

"My mom, no. My dad maybe. But I can't stress over it, it's not going to change anything. It's probably not good for the baby either. Talk to you later." I say as I give DJ a hug.

"Yeah talk to you soon."

"Hey mom, where is dad?"

"He is not here, he left, but how are you?"

"I'm okay, mom. I'm tired. I think I'm going to lay down."

"Okay Suesan, Gloria was looking for you." She yells as her voice carries upstairs.

Upstairs I see Gloria asleep in her bed. I give her a kiss and go into my room.

∽

PARTY!!! PARTY OVER HERE AND NOTHING OVER THERE WOOO WOOO. AAAAAAYYYYYYYYEEEEEEE!!! WOOO…WOOO!

So many people from school. So many people period, I thought to myself.

"Having lots of fun?"

"Hey Suesan, yes. Having lots of fun. And you?" Jahem asked this kissing me.

"Yes, any sign of Colton?" I asked looking around.

"No, haven't seen him." Jahem said, excitedly as he guided me to the dance floor.

"In just two days it'll be the beginning of summer break. Is this awesome or what?"

"Of course, but we have to get back, that's how school works."

"Two months plus an extra week is great. No?"

"You are absolutely right." Jahem said, as his face turned from joyful to serious. "Suesan, I am going to spin you around, look at the entrance and see who is there." Jahem said, as he turned me around to the entrance to see Colton.

"Who would have thought Jahem, the party is already two hours in, and he had to show up?" Jahem looked at me for my next move. "No my love, I am not running this time. We are going to stay right here."

"Okay good for you." Jahem said, beaming with pride. Jahem gave me a hug, then slowly pulled me away. "Your stomach." Jahem added, as he touched my stomach. "Not for nothing, but your stomach is bigger. Are you gaining weight?"

"No, Jahem why would you ask me a question like that?" I asked, as I pulled my sweater around my stomach.

"My mistake, just asking."

"Well no, it's not." I said as I took a step back and continued dancing.

"Okay, that's all you had to say. I didn't mean to offend you."

Colton made his way over to us dancing and interrupted our conversation. He was very close to us both. "Well, well, well here you two go dancing again."

"You want to dance with me?" Jahem asked Colton.

Colton looked at me and then looked back at Jahem. Everything I wanted to say to Colton was balling up into a big knot in my throat. The three of us stopped dancing on the floor. I couldn't breathe at the thought of him overhearing Jahem's suspicions of my growing belly.

"No, that's alright, continue. I don't mind sharing my girlfriend." Colton leaned in close to Jahem's face. "Don't get too close to her." Colton said as he looked at Jahem who stared Colton down until he finally looked at me again.

"Suesan has her own mind." Jahem looked back at Colton. "How close she gets to me is up to her."

Colton stepped close to Jahem to whisper, "You think you tough?" I walked in between Jahem and Colton to create distance.

"You want to see how tough I am? You've been in jail for a long time. Don't get it confused with being out here. Things have changed and so did I."

"Stop it, you two. Look Colton, Jahem just came over to say hi." I said waiting on him to concur. "Right Jahem?"

"Yeah, okay." Jahem added. Colton kissed me on the cheek and walked away. Jahem shook it off and continued. "Where's Doren?"

"He said he was coming. Oh there he is, speaking of him." I pointed to DJ, anything to not have to talk about the current situation.

"What's up man?" Jahem said giving DJ a pound.

"Nothing, is the party over?" DJ pondered looking around.

"No, not yet." Jahem said.

"It's over in three hours. Then tomorrow is graduation. Are ya'll excited?"

(Unison) "No."

"Come on why not?" I asked hitting both of them in the arms playfully

"I am not ready for college."

"I second that." Doren added.

"We have to keep in touch." I stated.

The party went on and everyone was still having fun. I am glad it was on the beach. It was the right kind of atmosphere.

I did not see Colton or signs that he was still around and that was a blessing.

The beach party was over. Everyone packed their towels and other belongings and left. Jahem and Doren walked me home.

The funny thing is there was no tension between us and that was good. I liked spending time with them, it helped my aching problems. It's crazy how things play out. My life's going to get better and it's not going to have Colton in it. Life has tried to break me. But if it does not kill me it will make me stronger.

∼

"Alright, class of 2000, you made it through some tough times in your life. Though all of you sitting here today have faced many growing pains with the pressure and the joys of high school, just know you are some of the brightest students with the brightest futures. You can achieve anything. There are three students this year who have went above and beyond expectations while attending Wilmington High. These three students have respectively pushed through their own adversities on the way to the top of their class.

"Before I pass out the certificates, I would like to say these three students have been the pinnacle of the phrase *I can*. They have been through it all. Most importantly, they will make it through it all going forward."

"First honors, Doren James."

"Second honors, Suesan Johnson."

"And last but not least, third honors, Jahem Thomas."

"About two years ago today, these three students were chosen to enter college early. They chose to stay. They said school was not meant to be rushed. I say they made the right choice. Please give a round of applause for our three prized Valedictorians."

Chapter Thirteen:

Knocking Down Walls

Jahem : Suesan

"Do you remember when we first met and you believed it would be hard to make friends because you were new and alone?"

"Yes. I remember. And here we are three years later, best friends and brothers." As I was speaking I was getting flashbacks of being awkward, lost on the lunch line, and sitting at a lunch table by myself. I look up at Doren. "You definitely have come through for me so many times. I can never thank you enough for that."

"Thanks, Jahem. But I never came through for you. You never needed my help. You had more potential than you thought you had. I'm just happy I was able to come along for the ride. And by the way, if anyone could have been the person to help me get through some of the things I went through, it was you."

"What happened before I met you guys?" Suesan asks putting on her glasses.

"Jahem actually saved my life on more than one occasion. There had been plenty of days when I would leave school and get jumped by a group of kids from school. They either said it was because I was flirting with one of their girls or I looked at one of them funny." DJ looks at Suesan. "We know what it was really about though. And every time I was in the middle of something, Jahem would be right there to have my back. They'd call him a traitor or spook or oreo. Y'know, because he was siding with the enemy and stuff. Sure, they didn't know any better. We didn't either at the time but we started hanging out together." DJ looks at me with his fist out. "But best friends are one in a million."

"There was this other time when we were getting out of school and when we turned the corner by the basketball courts, we both got popped in the face by some boys waiting for us. They ran off by the time we could even know what just happened, and then they threw rocks at his window while we were doing homework or playing Xbox at his house. DJ's mom would report it but we were well off school grounds and it seemed like the cops had other things that seemed more important."

"And from that day forward we knew we could only rely on each other. We have a bond like no other. It's like we sense each other." We laugh. "I told him, no matter what he needed—to just call me and I'll be there in a hurry. We are ready to fight for each other." DJ turns from Suesan to me. "We are brothers for life. I love you bro."

"I love you too."

"Wow. How times have changed. We all grew up haven't we?" Suesan asks looking at me.

"Yes times were tough but you know what, we made it. The feeling is so unbelievably incredible." Doren reminisces as he gulps the rest of his soda.

"Do ya'll want anything else to drink?" Suesan asks as

she gets up off the stoop of her house.

"Grape for me." I gesture with my finger.

"Orange." says Doren as he picks up his empty soda can and gives it to Suesan.

"Man, Doren" I hit Doren softly in the arm. "College, I am going to use the summer like it's no tomorrow." DJ shakes his head in agreement. "I want to return to Allentown for a while, so I can show the old neighborhood what I've become." I say laughing at my own success. "The last time I planned on going back was around the time Jaramia showed up. Since then I've been helping out and between that and school I was caught up. But now that chapter is closed and I can do just that."

Suesan came back with the sodas a couple of minutes later. She had to feed Dayla and take her out back to use the bathroom. At least the sodas were still ice cold.

"So is anyone getting cars?" I ponder.

"I'm getting one shortly." Suesan states.

"As for me, I don't know. I guess when the time is right. I am saving money. It's time for me to get a bit more serious about life." I'm sure DJ was still getting used to the idea of maturing so he changed the subject.

"Oh wow look at who's coming around the corner." DJ says annoyingly. We all look at DJ and we all say the name at almost the same time, "Colton."

"Why, why, why?" Suesan says to herself.

"Hey Suesan baby. I thought you would be home. Not with them two, but anyway…I brought you something."

"Thank you."

"Well you can thank me by giving me a kiss."

"Look, Colton I am tired okay."

"I don't think you are tired. You're not tired enough to be staying outside with them." Colton says but I can't tell if it's with disgust or hostility.

"Well, I am Colton. Sorry. Thanks for the gift, really. I'm just sitting down relaxing."

"It's just one kiss, Suesan."

"I think she just said no Colton." I tell him and I'm sure my eyes could cut flesh with the way I was looking at him.

"I don't care, Jahem. She's my girl, not yours. So mind your business."

"Won't ya'll two stop?" DJ says trying to get a handle on the situation. "She is her own person. She knows what she wants and we're all adults here."

"Come on give me a kiss." Colton says ignoring DJ and moving closer towards the steps.

"You've been drinking, Colton. Haven't you?" Suesan says stern but a bit worried. Colton is insisting on the kiss. He grabs Suesan's arm and my body gets flushed with heat. Suesan yells out for Colton to stop and he shouts "Where's my kiss?!?" And at this point DJ and I stand up and I shove Colton.

"Didn't she say no?!?" At this point, I am on the last step and he standing less than a foot away from me on the sidewalk.

"What, you want to fight? What do you care!?!"

"Okay cool, if you're fightin' then you gotta fight both of us then." Doren announces, calmly standing to crack his knuckles and fix his hoody.

"You're not going to give me a kiss?" Colton takes a step back and looks at Suesan, mouth agape.

"No, I'm not giving you a kiss. Step off, Colton."

"Fine. Then give me a hug." Colton says with a smirk as he reaches for her again. Suesan gives him a hug and I wish she wouldn't have given him the satisfaction. But then he opened his mouth on her lips and at that moment all rational thoughts were lost and I lunge forward with my right hand that leveled him. He got exactly what he deserved. I saw him kissing my girl. MY girl, not his anymore. I couldn't control my impulse. I was so angry.

Suesan moves behind us, and Doren and I are about shoulder to shoulder. Once Colton realizes what has happened he staggers to his feet. "I am leaving!"

"Fine... go to hell Colton." Suesan yells as she finds her voice to defend herself again.

"You go to hell, you dirty b--"

Doren stops him, "You better watch your mouth." Colton just waves at him dismissively and leaves down the block mumbling to himself.

"Jahem." Suesan says as she hits me from the back. "Do you think you should have punched him that hard? Or punched him at all? I would have slapped him myself. He would have been less aggressive if it was from me."

"Look I don't care. I don't care anymore." I haven't come down from my frustrations.

"Still, hold onto your patience, please. Regardless, thanks guys."

"You have to leave him. This has to stop." I'm looking into her eyes in a way I haven't before.

"I am. I just don't know when or how."

"After seeing what just went on I think the time has come." I proclaim.

Doren puts his hand on my shoulder, "Give her some more time." I give Suesan a kiss and say my goodbyes. DJ and I walk home.

∽

BARK BARK, chatters Dayla. "C'mon, let's go work out those little legs of yours. We're going to the park. Let's Go." Suesan zips up her lavender track jacket, leashes Dayla and leaves through the back of the house. After reaching the first corner and crossing the street, Suesan and Dayla break out into a light jog. Crossing onto the boardwalk, to continue jogging, Jahem sees them coming towards him while he sips a milkshake at an outside table. When the dog and owner are closer to Jahem, Dayla makes a b-line to a lamppost across the restaurant where Jahem is eating. Suesan stops but gives the leash a little tug, "This isn't the place to pee, sweetie."

"Why not, it's a free country." Jahem says getting up, hoping to surprise his love.

Suesan immediately recognizes the voice. "I know that's true." She turns around and waves her hands. "Are you catching a break too? I am." She asks.

Jahem throws his burger wrapper in the trash and walks over to her. "Well... um... I am, I need one, too." He says thoughtfully.

"What happened?" They interlock arms and Suesan gestures them to the swings while Dayla does figure eights around their legs.

"Jaramia is asking about his father and you know how complicated that must be. I'm sure my mom and father are done. And anyway, he's in jail and won't be coming out. And I also don't think she's ready to date yet, especially because they're still technically married." He stops talking for a second. "I try to be a good role model for him. I try to be a father figure and a loving brother at the same time. Am I not doing a good job?"

"Babe you're doing great. Everything will be okay. He's young. Like I said, you're doing a great job." Suesan reassures him by rubbing his back.

"But is it enough though? For him, I mean?"

"Do you want my honest opinion?"

"Of course. Always."

Suesan ties Dayla's leash to the pole of the swing set. "I know you are being a great brother and a strong male role model. To me, you two have developed a precious relationship and you spend a lot of time with him. I think what makes a good father is time. And you know this too, just the idea of being there makes an impact. No matter what, you will always love him and he will always love you, right? So don't worry about the rest. You're doing your best and that is what being a family is all about."

"That's not how you speak to me." Colton seems to have come from the other side of the park and was leaning up against another swing set with a lit cigarette in his mouth where his lip was still busted and bruised.

"Look COLTON! Jahem and I are not in the mood. So can you leave?"

"I don't care about Jahem. What's going on with you two?" Colton says, walking toward Suesan's side of the swing and taking another pull of the cigarette. He blows the smoke in her direction

"Don't, don't do that." Suesan says waving the smoke away. "Please leave." Colton doesn't move. "Look, you did this yesterday and you're doing it today. LEAVE. NOW. Before this gets any crazier."

"Look. I haven't heard anything about him being your boyfriend. I am. So let's take a walk." He holds his hand out to grab hers but she moves it away and steps off the swing. Jahem is now off of the swing, ready to fight but giving Suesan the chance to speak for herself.

"Girl, stop playing with me!" Colton reaches for both of her hands. Jahem realizes there's no talking to this guy, he lunges at Colton and they topple to the ground.

At this point, tensions have been brought to a boil and they're punching and kicking each other. Colton turns Jahem over from being on top of him but Jahem is able to scramble to his feet. All he could think about is Colton's busted lip as they locked up again and delivered several right hands to each other. "STOP!! STOP IT!! LET GO OF HIM!! JAHEM!! NO!!" Suesan is screeching and crying, Dayla was cowering and barking. This is bad.

Nothing she says stops the fists from flying. And this commotion is starting to draw a bit of a crowd. Some people are watching and some kids from the high school were there, too. Colton's left hand is at Jahem's throat and he is thrown against the wall but Jahem does not let up, continuously throwing hands to Colton's body and head. Suddenly a different body came into the circle. It's DJ and he rips Colton away from Jahem.

"You okay man?" Doren asks, fists clenched. Jahem nods his head as he wipes some of the blood off his lip. Though a bit shaken up, Colton recovers and is standing firm. He looks around at the people and then back at Suesan, Jahem, and DJ.

"REALLY? You defend HIM instead of ME." He directs this towards Suesan, beating his chest with each word. "Look at what you're doing!!" He goes into his pocket and draws a black and silver object. He clicks the button and a switchblade cuts the wind. The crowd gasps, some move away and Jahem and DJ take a step back but Suesan goes in front of them with her hands up.

"Please, Colton. Look at me. It's about time I tell you. I wasn't yours ever since you went to jail. I started hanging out with Jahem when you went to jail—in the beginning just as a friend. Then it escalated into something very special. He treats me good. I changed a lot because I'm around people who want what's best for me, people who love me and don't use me. I'm sorry, I can't let this go on any longer. I don't want any more fighting. I didn't want to tell you because I felt I had to hold on to the past." Suesan pauses to look at Jahem then back at Colton.

"Thank you for protecting me when you did but it is not right to keep you when time after time Jahem has proven himself to be a great person." Suesan looks at Jahem. "I caused this mess, and it wasn't fair for Jahem to wait for me to speak to you or for any of this to happen. Our chapter is over. I don't want us to be anything anymore. So don't bother me. You and I are through."

There was a long silence in that area of the park. DJ and Jahem look at each other because they know what they did was wrong. They also look at some of the people in the crowd, many of them with faces of shock and disappointment because now they all knew the big secret too. Jahem shakes his head and tells himself that he should never have supported the idea of Suesan and him while Suesan was with another man.

Suesan looks back to Jahem and grabs his hand. Suesan's words rang true and he too, realizes that he was the cause of this mess. Who was he, then just another thug like Colton? The couple looks at each other and then at Colton who is now standing erect but with his guard down, as a single tear streams down his cheek. This was the first time anyone saw this man break.

"This can't be true." Colton says, shaking his head.

"It is." Suesan confirms.

Sniffing in deeply, he closes his switchblade and puts it in his back pocket. "Okay. Alright. I won't be bothering ya'll anymore." With his head down he walks pass some of the remaining bystanders and leaves DJ, Jahem, and Suesan to their thoughts.

Chapter Fourteen:

Let Go

Jahem

There's a knock at the door that wakes me out of my sleep. I go downstairs and look out the window and I couldn't believe my eyes. How dare his punk ass come back after all he has done? Knock after knock, bell after bell, I heard him on the other side, "Hellooooo. I know ya'll are in there."

"Jahem, who is that?" My mom says coming down the stairs with a bit of upset in her voice.

"Go back up the stairs mom, I will take care of this."

"Jahem. Why are you talking like that? Who's at the door?" Mom says coming towards me and before I can tell her, she also looks out the window. "Oh my god. What is he doing here?" That upset turns to worry.

"I don't know."

"Take your brother and go upstairs." She says this with assertiveness but I don't move. "Jahem, you heard me. Now go!"

"Come on Jaramia." I gesture to Jaramia and grab his hand. I tell him to stay in his room and to not come out no matter what he hears.

"Why Jahem? You are scaring me."

"Don't be scared bro, just stay here, okay?"

"Okay. I love you."

I go back down to see mom talking to Doyle from behind the door.

It's cracked open far enough with the door chain on. Maybe about 6 inches. After Doyle went away, the chain was put on the door just as a precaution. As far as we knew, he wasn't coming back, or if he did, it wouldn't have been this quickly.

At the door I can hear him, "Let me in or I will bust down the door." My mom's voice wavers as she's yelling back, asking him to go or she will have to call cops. I call for her and she angrily turns her head to tell me to get the hell upstairs.

I can't. My fists are clenched as I stand at the middle of the staircase.

"Is that Jahem? Son, come open this door for your old man." I imagine he's trying to poke his head in as if I can't hear him. He really thinks I give a damn about him.

"No, Doyle. You have to leave. Now."

"What? You disobeying my orders? But I'm your father."

"My mom and I will call the cops and you will get arrested. Don't put us through this."

"Look, please. I just want to talk." He says with some sense of calm.

"Are you sure?" Mom asks.

"Yes. I'm sure."

"If anything goes wrong you are leaving immediately."

"That's fine. Like I said, I just want to talk. And to apologize."

After a moment she unhooks the chain and lets him in. He steps inside the house, looking around to see how it has changed. He seems to be scanning the house, getting a feel of the layout, recalling his older history when this was, in fact, his house, though it hasn't been for a long time now.

He himself looks more muscular than he ever did before. The scar on his face creates the illusion that he is scarier than I've known him to be. My mom left a mark that will forever remind him of what he lost. He walks in as if nothing happened, and as if this is his first time being here. His eyes shift back and forth like he's to be aware of every detail and everyone. I don't know how my mom is feeling, but he will never hurt her again.

As he is walking into the living room he was getting ready to have a seat and mom told him to not make himself comfortable. He didn't listen and sat down anyway and stared at me.

"Jahem. Look how you've grown. Come and sit next to your pa."

"Leave that boy alone. You said you wanted to talk."

"Well, I don't want to talk too much now. At least, not yet. Let me enjoy this couch for a little bit. It's been a long time that I haven't been in my house and it feels really good to be inside it again."

"Well, that can't be here. I think you've already overstayed your welcome as a guest. This is no longer your home with you in it."

"No. As far as I know, this is still my house. If this is my house, then this is under my control." He declares as he sits back and puts his feet up on the coffee table.

"Get out or we will call the cops." I tell him standing tall by the threshold of the door. The last time he saw me there, I was a lot shorter. A lot younger. I'm not that boy anymore. I am not afraid.

"I would not do that if I was you, son." Doyle throws his right arm over the top of the couch cushion and sinks his back deeper into the couch. His bubble jacket spreads out more to reveal a gun tucked into the side of his pants.

He stretches, but I know this is a part of this sick act. "Hmm... You think I wanted to talk? No. You are mistaken. I want you to hurt. Do you see what you did to my face? Do you see what you did to my legs? You did this to me and now you are going to pay." Suddenly his demeanor shifts and he stands up as quick as he could. "But this time you will not leave me like you did before. No. This time... you will die." He draws the gun from his waist and points it at mom.

She whimpers and throws her arms up. "I didn't leave you, Doyle. You left me. You continuously chose drinking over me." Even in this situation, she's still one of the bravest people I know, still managing to have a sense of calm as she slowly steps in front of me.

"Look, I have kids that need me. You can't do this, Doyle."

"Kids? As far as you and I are concerned we've only had one child and he's right there all grown up." He smiles and looks at me, then back at mom. "So he doesn't need you anymore."

"I... I have another son. He needs me."

"Yeah. That son you lied about. The one that you told me was mine. The same son that was supposed to be dead, but you left him with Franco. That—FUCK you cheated on me with." Doyle pats himself on the temple with the nose of the gun and looks at me as he puts the gun down. "Did you know about that, Jahem? That your mother is no better than me. How she FUCKED another man while we were married. While I was working for all of this." He spins around with his arms up. "THIS WHOLE HOUSE exists because of me. YOU exist because of ME."

By this point, he is walking around the room and mom and I are keeping our distance from him. Now we're both equal distances from the threshold into the hallway. It was a stalemate, there was no running. His eyes look like they're about to pop out of their sockets, I've never seen him like this. "Jahem, did you know she moved here to get closer to that damn child? The one that she's NEVER been a mother to? She waited for her opportunity to move here."

He looks back at my mom and points his gun at her again. "And you say that Madison is a manipulator? At least when I was married to her, she was 100% honest with me--" Doyle seems to have stopped mid-sentence. He takes a deep breath and wipes his eyes with the back of his hand and chuckles. "Madison says tears are for the weak. Now, where was I? Oh yeah. So this is a farewell." He cocks the gun.

KNOCK….KNOCK…KNOCK. There were blue and red lights flashing through our window blinds.

"IT'S THE WILMINGTON POLICE. Come out with your hands up!"

"Who in the hell called the cops?" He looks at us and then the stairs where he notices a little boy kneeling down looking down at us. "JARAMIA!" Doyle howls as he began to run for the stairs with hate in his eyes. Jaramia shrieks and runs up the stairs. With all of my might I run towards Doyle, tucking my head and bracing my shoulder for the biggest impact of my life.

As my body connects to his I feel both pairs of our feet go airborne before hitting the hardwood of the hallway and a shot rang out. I immediately grab his hands but there was no gun and just then the police busted into the house. I'm thrown off of Doyle and they pile on top of him, yoking him up into handcuffs.

After we tell Jaramia how smart he was for calling the cops, I tell my family that I love them and I was going to go take a walk to clear my head. I decide to visit Suesan to explain to her what just happened.

"I can't believe he came back, Jahem. I'm glad everyone is alright."

"Luckily Jaramia knew who to call. That kid has been through so much. I just want to do right by him. It's so crazy. I really thought I was going to lose my mom today."

Suesan hugs me and kisses me on the forehead. "You're so special and brave Jahem. And so is Jaramia. Your mother has made some very special men."

"Do you want to go inside?"

"No, it feels good out here." We relax for a short time before I realize that my day isn't going to get easier yet. We see Colton coming down the block and we get up from the bench on the sidewalk to quickly go inside Suesan's house.

Colton starts to walk faster when he sees us retreating and he's already too close. "YO. I KNOW YOU SEE ME COMING. WAIT UP. Well, well, look who we have here. The girl that left me and the guy she left me for. Is this wonderful or what?"

"Look Colton, leave us alone!" Suesan says heatedly. "We dealt with a lot today. So we don't need you adding any more drama."

"No?" Colton says as he walks around us to block out the path towards Suesan's house. Just then I notice some of his gang come from around the corner. It's a setup.

"Word, Colton? So you couldn't just squash this after the other day?" This can't get us out of this situation but it's the best I got.

"I told you I won't cause any more problems, but I didn't say I won't be bringing any more problems with me."

One of the members of the Tuff Boys, wearing a hoodie steps forward, "Hello Suesan. Remember me?"

"If you're a part of Colton's group, of course I know you."

"Na, I'm not from this group. Look even closer. Into my eyes. I think you will remember me." Jason says pulling down his hood.

"I don't know what you are talking about."

"Oh, I think you know. Think 8th grade and places you shouldn't be. A wild night of drinking and sex. An abandoned house. One room. Hmph, maybe you don't remember… But I do." He has the most devilish grin I've ever seen. This day just kept getting darker.

I look to Suesan and her eyes are empty. Her hands are clammy and hot in mine and her face is flushed under tears. It takes me a second to realize the tremors in her fingers and then I could see that she was actually shaking. She takes a step back and clasps her mouth letting out a guttural cry. I hold her.

"What the hell is going on?!?" I say pissed. I'm done with these guys.

"Well, why don't you just ask her, pretty boy?" Jason gives me a head nod as he clasps his hands by his jean zipper. The rest of the group is snickering, including Colton. "You ain't her first, lover boy. Ask her what we did all night long. Ask her!"

"It's you!" She screams. "Get away! I'm going to call the damn cops on you!!!" She's shrieking and trying to get out of my arms, but I can't let her. She's too unstable and I'm still trying to get a handle on things. With tears falling from her eyes, she continues, "It was you that night! And you knew who I was! You knew I was drunk and just had a fight with Colton, how could you!?" Her voice is trailing off.

My body is starting to fill with a familiar heat I got from looking at Colton. I have my eyes dead set on him. "And you knew about this whole thing, Colton? What kind of man are you?"

"Knew about it? I was in on it." Here I am, just standing here and holding my girl. I'm so confused and hurt, I can't imagine the pain Suesan is feeling. I try to speak up but I can't even register what I'm saying. "Sweet, sweet Suesan. I knew this whole time and I am okay with that. I didn't know that when you left that night he was following you. But when he told me the next day that you were so drunk you didn't even question what was going on, I knew my revenge worked." I couldn't believe this, but Colton gestures at Jason for him to continue.

"Good ol' Colton here slipped some roofies in your beer when you weren't looking." Jason says through his smile.

"And seeing how we turned out, I don't regret what happened between the two of you one bit. I always knew you were too loose."

Suesan drops to her knees. "How can you do this to me, Colton? I thought you loved me." Suesan cries out.

"That's enough!" I get out my phone to call the cops. And the group rushes me. I swing at them and catch one or two but I lose my footing and get pushed to the ground, feeling the bottoms of sneakers and boots slam on my head, torso, and legs. Even through this commotion, I hear Suesan scream out my name and Jason say, "Nuh-uh, you're coming with us."

The crowds of feet stop and I collect myself to see Jason struggling to hold onto Suesan, who is attempting to fight him off. With all my strength I get up to charge the group but Colton stops me with the flip of his blade. "Come closer and I'm going to gut you." He threatens. He grabs Suesan's hair and pulls her head back and forth a few times and waves the knife in her face, "Keep squirming and I got something for you, too."

"I'm not going!" Suesan screams.

I can't stand this! I put my hands up and stand as firm as my mother did back home, but it's different when your lip is already leaking on your shirt. "Listen! LISTEN! This is crazy, STOP! Holding on to this resentment and pain is not going to help you get anything you want. Not like this!"

"Really, Jahem? Don't you see that I'm about to go back to jail? If it isn't for this it'd be something else. It's just a matter of time for someone like me. I might as well take one of you or both of you down with me. What do I have to lose? Jahem! You took everything from me."

"Colton, just slice'em and let's go." Jason says irritated. "YEEEEAOOOW!" Suesan bites Jason's arm and he puts her down struggling and she gets free. Just then, one of the Tuff Boys tries to catch Suesan and bumps into Colton and he drops the knife by me and I pick it up. As Suesan runs toward the house with Jason in hot pursuit. I step in front of him and the crowd. With the momentum of his running, he wrestles me to the ground with my hands on his jacket, we come down hard on her front lawn. I feel my right hand sink into his chest and I know what just happened.

In the commotion, Colton and the others stop and start freaking out. I hear so many *yo*'s and *what the hell*'s and *aww shit*'s on top of each other, and I get out from under a coughing Jason whose squirming with eyes wide. My right hand is moist and warm and the sight of the blood almost makes me faint. Colton is kneeling down by Jason, telling him to fight through it and get up before the cops come but Jason couldn't move. "Awww shit, awww shit. This is bad. This dude needs to get taken care of."

I'm frozen on the lawn. I can't believe how this has escalated. I'm proud that I've protected Suesan today. The best way I could've. But I still don't feel good. I'm sitting here, with my pants and shirt dirt-crusted along with drying blood stains that could be mine or someone else's. And I just watch how a group of boys can be so animalistic; in a harsh display of survival that we brought upon ourselves.

Colton's anger grew. Now he's huffing and puffing. He reaches into Jason's jacket and pulls out a small glock. By the time I was coming back from my own thoughts he was standing up and pointing the gun at me.

"One of my brothers is dying here, Jahem. Now I am going to kill you." Before he could pull the trigger, cop sirens were heard in the distance. Colton looks around at his group and then Jason on the floor and hesitates. "Damnit, it's the cops! We gotta split!" And within 10 seconds, they were all over fences, across yards, and down different streets. By the time the squad cars pull up, I was in my same spot, just feet away from Jason, who was barely breathing.

∼

Suesan and I told them everything, the whole truth. Everything. An ambulance was called as well as Jason's parents and my mom. Suesan's parents soon showed up too. I was very scared that I was in deep trouble. I would have never imagined that I was capable of stabbing someone.

After the questioning, we were getting seen by the paramedics. I was in pain and my face didn't look too good, but I didn't feel like going to the hospital. "You okay, Suesan? I'm so sorry all of this has happened. All of it. I'm here for you."

"I know you are. And yes… yes I am okay." She said this wincing, as she applied some ice to the back of her head. "My head just hurts." She put her head on my shoulder as we sat at the end of an ambulance truck. "I love you, Jahem. Thank you for saving me."

"No. I love you, thank you for saving me. You did a great job back there."

"But what are we going to do about Colton?" Suesan said worried.

"Don't worry about Colton. The cops are on it. Just worry about going in the house and resting up. I'll drive my mom home then come back and stay with you until you go to sleep."

Chapter Fifteen:

You Are Mine

Jahem

"You been stuck in the house for two weeks now. It's time for you to go out and enjoy yourself. Get some fresh air. I understand a week, but two weeks is crazy. Go breathe, and take Suesan with you. Both of ya'll need some air. Clarissa called me and said Suesan isn't getting out much either. I know you both might be being cautious but the police are sure to handle it. Besides staying in the house is what he would want."

"Maybe you're right mom." I told her as I leaned on the headboard of my bed. "I'll get dressed and call Suesan. Maybe I'll even invite DJ.

"Thank you. It would do you some good." My mom said, as she patted my leg and walked out of my bedroom.

I called up Suesan and Doren and we all agreed to go to the skating rink. I told them I would pick them up in the afternoon. Jaramia overheard the conversation and wanted to go, but I didn't want to worry about him when Colton shows up everywhere uninvited.

～

I arrived at Suesan's house first to spend some alone time with her. I haven't spoken to her as much as we used to for these two weeks seeing how hard it was for us to deal with Jason's death. The funeral was just the other day and we were both still shaken up. We texted but it's nothing like hearing her voice every day. On our way to pick up DJ, we talked about the day Jason died and how we are moving passed it and looking forward to spending more time with each other. Suesan vented to me that it's not easy for her still seeing the blood stain he left. For some reason, it just hasn't washed away. "I keep on reliving the night of his death, and just like seeing the whole thing from the window. I felt so helpless in that situation." I reassured her that we will get through this trauma eventually, with the help of each other.

We arrived at DJ's house and waited for him to come downstairs. After he checked in on us he started to break the ice the way he knew best, joking about random things. We knew what he was doing but he was a good friend. Suesan and I laughed and joked with him, and it felt like old times. It felt good for me to laugh and think about other things besides the fact that I am technically a murderer. Life is funny, too. I took a life in self-defense, and others seem to think that it was justified. I, on the other hand, seem to be the only person blaming myself. But right now I felt joy again and it is thanks to my brother and the woman I love.

∽

Wilmington has a lot of skating rinks, but we drove to Oleander Dr., the most famous of the Wilmington skating rinks. It's a family fun rink with a hockey area on the other side. We had a great time but I still felt this darkness in the pit of my stomach. I assumed it was just the way I was dealing with these issues. We waited for the very last song to play and gave back our rented skates. The person at the register graduated from our same high school so we were all talking to her for a little while. It was really nice to be out again and I noticed we were one of the last ones to leave it seemed, aside from some of the workers.

Leaving for the parking lot though, I got those stomach sensations again when I saw what I did. Leaning up against my car was Colton. He threw up his hands and I heard footsteps rushing towards us. It was his crew and they had us surrounded. We were trapped again. I didn't let him see my fear but I prayed for a miracle.

"Suesan you think you can run from me?" Colton said this in what he thought was a beloved tone. "You were never brave Suesan, remember? That is why I was there." Colton's face turned from adoration to hatred. As he entered the circle, just feet away from us. He drew a gun and held back the tears in his eyes. "You had me!" He yelled to Suesan, as he pointed it to his chest where his heart lied.

"Colton." I softly called to him, as I slowly stepped forward to stand in front of Suesan. DJ followed suit to put Suesan in between us. "Suesan has been brave for a long time. But sometimes we have to understand that it is alright to ask for help. We can never be too full of pride or privilege to ask for help when we need it. Colton, Suesan does not want to be yours anymore. She doesn't need your protection. She is not afraid anymore. But it is okay to ask for help. We already had someone else die. We can stop it right now." I explained as calm as possible.

"It's funny how life plays out." Colton stated, as he looked up to the sky and tapped his gun by his side.

"What you mean, Colton?" Suesan asked, as she walked from in between DJ and me.

"Jahem, did Suesan tell you about the depth of our relationship?"

"Anything dealing with Suesan I already know. We don't keep secrets." I looked at Suesan. "I know exactly what is going on. She is bound to you in ways we both know is not right. I don't care what you both agreed to, she wants out of it. She is done."

∼

Well, she is not leaving me." Colton looks at Suesan. "Suesan, you are leaving him. You are mine, till death do us part." Colton declared as he switches his eyes from me to Suesan. "Either you come with me and spare Jahem, or I kill him. But either way, you are coming."

"Look Colton, I love Suesan, okay? And she loves me. Suesan has her own decisions to make at this point. Don't you want her to be happy?"

He's crying a bit more. Between tears, he says, "Did, Suesan, tell you who Gloria is to her?" Colton asks as his gun is trembling. "No one knows except her parents and I. Why do you think they kept me around? Do you think they would otherwise?" Colton says with a smirk on his face. DJ and I look at Suesan, who looks very nervous.

"Colton, don't do this." Suesan says slowly in agony. Tears start to form in her eyes as she stares at Colton.

"Jahem when-"

"Wait Colton." Suesan cries out. "Jahem, Gloria is not my sister. Gloria is my daughter." I felt my face transform. Her eyes fixed on Colton.

"Yes Jahem, her daughter." Colton states with a grim smile. "But she didn't tell you that. Right, Jahem?"

"Were you going to tell me?" I ask Suesan, as she looks down to avoid my eyes. I sound a bit strong in my voice. At this point, I couldn't tell what I was angry about. "I rather have found out from you. You know that." I say in a loud whisper, choking on my salty tears. "Colton. I don't know what you seek to accomplish by humiliating her. I still feel the same way about her. Nothing has changed." DJ puts his hand on Suesan who looks back at him.

"Is it Colton's child?" DJ asks. "Or is it Jason's, Suesan?" She was frozen. "Suesan. Please."

Suesan looks at Colton then at me and DJ. She says quietly, "I didn't know who it was until the other day. It's Jason's child." Fresh new tears poured from her eyes. I pull Suesan in for a strong hug.

"It's going to be alright."

"Jahem, I am sorry I didn't tell you."

"It's alright, Suesan." I look at Colton. "I still love her. I'm going to be there for her. We're bonded, Colton."

"DAMN IT!" Colton says lifting his gun again. "HOW?!? There is not that much love in the world to stay with her after what you've heard. I thought for sure that you'd GIVE SUESAN BACK TO ME!"

"No. Colton. She is not some object you can own. This is the problem. We can get through this. Put the gun away and we can get you guidance and help."

"What do you know about ANYTHING, Jahem? I was away for

TWO YEARS. For 2 years I wanted to kill you. Since I was in jail I knew you and Suesan was sneaking around. You both were so obvious." He looks at Suesan. "But I thought it was some phase to get me jealous. Just because you both were smart. Maybe you needed to get it out of your system. Maybe it was because I was away and you felt unsafe. No one will protect you like I have."

Suesan steps in front of me. I could sense a different energy in her. She was losing the battle of calm in her head. She stomps her foot down. "You call what you have done to me protecting me? You have ruined my life COLTON. You never protected me. I feared life then and now. You let another man have their way with me. I HAD A BABY BECAUSE YOU COULDN'T CARE ENOUGH. You just controlled me and created fear in my heart. I needed you and you failed." Suesan wipes her eyes and takes another step away from me. The circle around us widened. "You used me, so you can BURN. IN. HELL!" Suesan takes my hand and starts to walk away.

"This is your problem. You don't see all the good I do for you. Well, this will be your final lesson." He cocks it. DJ and I step forward but his goons grab us up and throw us to the ground. I felt helpless. I've wrapped up so many of my loved ones into my problems. Now DJ and I are getting pummeled on the gravel.

"You want to know what the funny thing is?" He says this loud so DJ and I can hear this even through the ruckus of being beaten. There's only one bullet in this gun. It may not be for you today, Suesan. But if not today, then tomorrow or the next day..."

At this point, I can't feel my body and I'm sure DJ can't either. In and out of it, I'm held up into a seated position, I see that DJ is held up in a similar way. We're positioned to look at Suesan and Colton. He's ghastly and she's scared but glowing. I know that there have been wars waged over women so beautiful. And there she was, a true Helen of Troy.

"...And even if you find a way to trick us all again and stay alive, I hope that you are dead inside. Final time then Suesan. Your last chance: are you coming?"

"……… No……"

He switched from holding the gun in Suesan's direction and he pointed it at me. "Jahem. Say hi to hell for me.

One….. Two…. Three…"

BANG….. ……. ………. ……. ….. ………..

And all I remember was the sound of feet and one body hitting the ground.

Chapter Sixteen:

You Will Be Missed

Jahem

I arrived at the hospital holding Suesan, calling out for any doctors to help. My clothes are soaked with her blood. Everything happened so fast. I kept talking to Suesan to keep her eyes fixed open on me. She went in and out of consciousness as the doctors laid her down on the gurney. The doctors asked me what happened, we all looked a bit banged up. All I could do was look at her. DJ spoke up and answered all of the doctor's questions through a swollen cheek.

I just held Suesan's hand and kept telling her to squeeze as hard as she could, until they told me that I had to wait in the waiting room as they took her away. I couldn't move. I stood frozen. My heart was ripped from my soul the moment the bullet ripped through her. DJ grabbed me into a hug. That hug was all I needed to release all the built up pressure and hurt I felt inside. I started to cry as if my eyes were a faucet. We stood there a very long time before DJ moved me into the waiting area. I zipped up my sweater to hide the blood on my shirt.

The wait felt like forever. DJ and I called our family including Suesan's and let them know what had occurred. Everyone arrived in the blink of an eye. It's unfortunate that they were getting used to these kinds of things. DJ and I were surrounded by everyone we loved and now we were just waiting for the doctor. The doctor came hours later to tell us that Suesan recovered. He reassured everyone that Suesan was in stable condition and resting. She lost a lot of blood so they had to keep her overnight for observation.

Later on, I was greeted by the same doctor. He asked me if I wanted to see her. Although I wanted to see her, her parents had more of a right than I did so I let them go first. When they came out they told me Suesan wanted to see me. I slowly stepped into her room as Suesan wiped her puffy eyes. She doesn't have to be strong for me, or for anyone else. She is already brave. I walk slowly to her and grabbed her hands. We both locked eyes and immediately started crying together. I sat at the chair next to her and leaned in for a kiss.

"I can't believe you jumped in front of a bullet for me." I said assertively. "You don't ever do a thing like that ever again." I tried to talk through the lump in my throat. "Don't save my life again, please. You have people who need you."

Suesan just smiled at me and caressed my face. "The doctor said every part of me is perfect. Every part." Tears continued to fall from her eyes. "I love you and I would do it again if it was to save your life. People need you too."

"I don't know what I'd do if I lost you. This was so scary." I said pleading with her.

I called DJ after we had our time. He walked in slower than I did towards Suesan. He swallowed hard and grabbed her other hand. He just stared at her with tears falling from his face.

"Did the doctor say that you are still healthy? Nothing else needs to be handled with you?" DJ pondered, as he sat on Suesan's bed.

"As I told Jahem, every part of me is healthy. I just have a patch over my chest. When that heals, I'll be perfect. Nothing else was affected by the bullet." Suesan stated in a bit of pain but relieved.

The next day I picked up Suesan to take her home. Her family was waiting for her with a large spread of food and was happy to see her. We sat them down and both explained the recent events to them, a bit during brunch but mostly in the living room afterward. They were not happy to know that Jason was really the father of Gloria because they thought Colton was the father. Suesan never told them about the rape. They wanted to call the cops on Colton but the cops had no trace of him ever since I took Suesan to the hospital. The cops located some of the Tuff Boys but they wouldn't dare tell them where he is hiding.

~

After we finished talking, Suesan and I went up to her room and I stayed over to make sure Suesan was okay. I don't know if I did it for her benefit or mine. Lucky for us, we had time to be in each other's arms. It was quickly over when Gloria started to cry. Suesan brought Gloria into the room and looked at me. I scooted over to the edge of the bed and patted the space next to me. Gloria reaches her hands out for me to hold her. I looked at Suesan as she sat down to give me Gloria. "So your daughter, and not your sister? I know why you felt the need to hide Gloria from the rest of the world. But I don't understand why you had to hide her from me."

Suesan kept staring. "I don't fault you if you are upset with me. I just didn't want to ruin things between us. I never found the right time to tell you."

"I am not upset at all Suesan. I just want to be a part of everything you are." I reached for Suesan's hand. "You are a mom. Regardless of what happened, Gloria is who is important, and the bravery you have shown to raise her is admirable."

"I'm not brave. I love my daughter but I didn't show that by lying."

"You protected her. In my book, that is the ultimate bravery a mother can show. You don't have to do this on your own. I will be on this ride with you." I gave Suesan a hug, then returned Gloria to her. "I didn't know if I can be who Jaramia needed me to be, but you believed in me, and that helped me believe in myself. Let me do the same for you. I believe-- no. I know, we will make great parents for Gloria. Don't hide anymore." I looked at Gloria then at Suesan. "You have a lot of support. And love. It's us against the world. I'll be everything Colton was and wasn't for you."

Gloria started crying again, so we moved our focus onto her. We played with every toy Gloria had in her room, and I am enjoying the life that Suesan and I are creating. The light at the end of the tunnel is shining brighter than it ever had before. As the evening came to an end, Suesan made plates of spaghetti for us to eat and I helped to feed Gloria. Once everyone ate, we laid in Suesan's room with Gloria in the middle. I looked over at Suesan then at Gloria as they drifted off to sleep and I felt the greatest peace. Without knowing, I created my own family. I am not a reflection of Doyle. I am a reflection of myself.

~

I woke up to Gloria in my arms. Gloria and Suesan were both sleep. I didn't want to wake Suesan so I slowly moved away and wrote a note to her with the paper I saw on her dresser. I told her that I loved her that and I'll see her later. I went home to shower and checked on my mom and brother. We talked, ate, and laughed. Later that day, there was a knock at the door. To my surprise, it was DJ with Suesan. I opened the door to board games and very energetic friends. It was around 2 o' clock when they came, and we had an amazing time. After we played so many different games, we ordered pizza and rented movies. By this time my mom and Jaramia joined us.

Everyone grabbed a slice or two and decided on a movie. It was just movies, pizza, and love the entire time until nightfall. We all said our goodbyes and I dropped everyone off. When I dropped Suesan off, she gave DJ a hug. She turned to me and said the most confusing thing to me, "We will always love you, Jahem." I grabbed Suesan hands before she had time to walk away. I questioned her choice of words.

"Shush now." Suesan walked towards me to kiss me. "You will have to trust me. You will see in time, if you haven't already." Suesan softly whispered. She opened the door to her house, and I closed the door behind her. As I closed my car door, I turned to DJ who was looking out the window. I know he feels my eyes on him but he doesn't say anything. Neither did I because in the back of my mind I wasn't ready to know.

For the past two days I had been enjoying my family and by now I've established a larger one, with DJ's and Suesan's. I'm glad we all found each other. Some people do not know the importance and meaning of love. There is not a force stronger than it, especially when it's unconditional. You can't choose some of your family, but you can make a family with others you love. And with that, nothing in the whole world can tear my love from those that are dear to my heart and soul.

I thought to myself that two days have passed and I did not hear from Suesan nor Doren. So I thought I might call them. Keeping up with this extended family sometimes got difficult too, but they understand. I tried to call Suesan so many times, but I couldn't get through. So I decided to call her house phone.

"Hello Ms. Johnson. I haven't heard from Suesan for two days, and I was wondering if she home now. She usually calls me if I don't call her."

"Jahem..." Ms. Johnson whispered my name. As much as she tried to hold back the breaking of her voice I felt uneasiness settle over me. Not again.

"Ms. Johnson... what's wrong with Suesan?"

"Colton shot Suesan last night in front of our house. We rushed her to the hospital...." She began to sob heavily. "But this time she didn't make it." Ms. Johnson started to uncontrollably cry out. "I...I told. Her. Not. To. Talk...to him." Ms. Johnson blew her nose. "But she didn't listen. She thought if she spoke to him alone that she can convince him to leave the two of you alone and turn himself in. She just wanted to be free, Jahem." Ms. Johnson paused to clear her throat. "I heard Colton say *I can't hold on if wounds remain*. Then the gun went off. Her father and I came outside to see our baby on the ground. She wasn't breathing or moving. The doctor pronounced her dead on arrival...my baby..... her 18th birthday was next week."

"Ms....Ms. Johnson...I'm, I'm..." I couldn't talk. I couldn't breathe. I sat my body on my bed. I knew if I continued to stand I would faint.

Suesan's father got on the phone. "Jahem, I'm sorry, but listen.... listen well. This is not your fault. It's Colton fault. Suesan loved you more than she showed you. The last memory you shared with her, she held on to that. She talked about game night and Gloria until I couldn't take it anymore. Now it's your turn to keep every memory you have of her in your heart and mind. You don't ever let go. I can never thank you enough for how you treated my daughter. You will forever be my son. These kids— they look up to you. My door will always remain open to you. She will forever look over you from above.

"Thank you, Mr. Johnson." I pushed out of my mouth. I sat frozen thinking about Suesan and everything we went through to be together. Then I remember, her last words to me, *we love you*.

"Mr. Johnson, did Suesan leave me anything? Last time I saw her, instead of her saying *I love you*, she said *we love you*. She told me to trust her and I'll find out what she meant…I guess I never will from her. Do you know?"

"Jahem." Mr. Johnson said seriously. "After you left that day she told us about Colton and Jason, she told us that she is pregnant by you. I thought you knew."

"No…no I did not." I stated as I lost all sense of feeling and time. I felt my heartbeat. I felt my heart rip piece by piece every time I breathe until it hurt to inhale. I cried and cried. Her belly. It all made sense now.

"Jahem." Mr. Johnson whispered. It snapped me back to reality. "I am going to the funeral home with the pastor. I can sure use some company. Clarissa is not doing so well with our baby gone. Would you come with me?"

"Yes. Yes, I'll come right over."

I hung up with him and went into my mother's room. I told her what I just found out, and she started to cry which made me cry again. She held me close and told me that I will eventually heal. She kissed me on the cheek and told me she loved me. I told her that I am going with Suesan's father to plan the funeral. My mom walked me downstairs and gave me one more goodbye hug.

"I love you mom." I said as I released her. She opened the door and froze. I saw the look of horror in her face. I turned to look outside to what she saw.

"YOU CAN'T RUN NOW, CAN YOU!" Colton said standing on the steps of my house.

"Don't Colton. Think before you do this. It's over. Suesan is gone. I don't have her now, and neither do you. Now put the gun away. You w--"

POW!

POW!

POW!

I landed hard on the ground. I open my eyes to a lot of blood on me. I patted my body but I wasn't in pain. The blood wasn't mine. I wasn't shot. I felt a hand grab my shirt. I turned to see my mom lying next to me. Jaramia came pounding down the stairs and he was screaming the loudest I've ever heard him. I couldn't understand what was going on. I leaned over my mom as her eyes were flittering. She just looked up. I looked outside the door, and I did not see Colton, he was gone. I called out for someone to call the ambulance. I looked down at the wound and took my sweater off to apply pressure on the hole in her chest.

"Jahem...protect...Jaramia...You...Are...All... He...Has...I love you, my sweet boy...I'm so sorry. I love you." Jaramia was holding her shoulder at this point telling her to wake up, wake up, wake up.

"Mom help is coming. You have to open your eyes. Please stay with me...Mom? Mom? MOM!" She was heavy.

And we sat there with her, both rocking her saying "We love you mom.... We love you..... Mom, please... We love you..... We love you...."

Printed and bound by PG in the USA